The Haunted

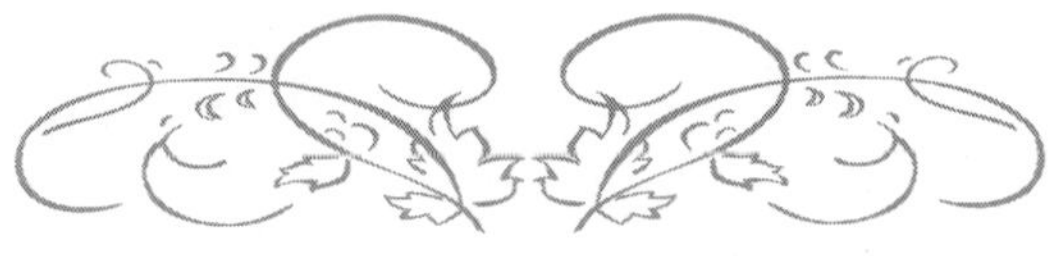

A MacKinnon Curse Novel

The Haunted: A MacKinnon Curse novel, book Two by J. A. Templeton

ISBN 9781480180505

1 Psychic Ability-Fiction 2. Ghosts-Fiction 3-Horror-Fiction 4. Love-Fiction
5. Supernatural-Fiction 6. Self-mutilation-Fiction

Cover Illustration by Kimberly Killion
Cover Photograph by Amanda Johansen
Editing by Bulletproofing
Formatting by Tracy Cooper-Posey

The Haunted

A MacKinnon Curse Novel

Book 2

J.A. Templeton

To Kip Brandon—
For having the ambition and fortitude to go after your dreams.
Son, I am so incredibly proud of you.

Chapter One

"*I will never leave you alone. Unless you forget about Ian MacKinnon. Forget about him, Riley, and I shall leave you and your family in peace. I will kill those you love if you continue.*"

Laria's warning to me before I'd broken the curse that had bound Ian's spirit to the world of the living rang over and over in my ears. I knew for a fact I had crossed Ian over. I had proof of that...especially since both my mom and Ian had visited me afterward. I had also seen Laria being led out of the castle dining room by a spirit, a man who I assumed was her father. So if I'd broken the curse, then why was she here, standing thirty feet away, staring at me like she wanted to kill me?

"How about that ride?" Kade asked, and I glanced at him, forcing a smile.

Kade reminded me so much of Ian with his shaggy dark hair and brilliant blue eyes. Everything about him, from his tall, athletic build to the grin and dimples, was spot on.

I wish Ian were here now. Granted, I was glad we had broken the and loafers, and I adored her. "How was your first day of school, my dear?"

"Good," I said, sliding my backpack off my shoulders.

"I knew you'd do just fine," she said, sounding pleased. "Are you hungry?"

"I might have a snack in a little bit. Megan's coming by at four to pick me up. We're gonna hang out for a while." I refrained from telling her about the glen, knowing she wouldn't be thrilled to hear I was partying in the woods with my new friends.

"I need to drop by and pick up the mail," she said, untying her apron. "I'll make you a snack when I get back."

A part of me wanted to ask her to stay until my friend Megan got here, but I didn't want to worry her or let on that anything was wrong. "Thanks, Miss A."

I walked up the steps, my legs feeling as heavy as lead. Taking a right at the top of the stairs, I stared at the door to my room, nervous to go in. Who or what was waiting for me inside? My hand actually trembled as I turned the doorknob and stepped inside.

I released the breath I'd been unconsciously holding.

My room was completely trashed.

Papers, books—basically everything that wasn't nailed down was on my bedroom floor. The comforter had been ripped from my bed, and in the middle of my mattress sat a matchbox.

A familiar matchbox that I knew with a certainty held my razor blades.

The hair on my arms stood on end. No way. I had thrown that matchbox away when Ian was still here.

Crossing the room, I snatched the matchbox off the bed, opened it up...and the blades spilled onto the mattress.

Do it.

The female voice rang in my ears, over and over, a chant that grew louder by the second.

You know you want to.

Laria was right. There was a part of me that craved the release of cutting, but I had promised myself, Shane and Ian that I wouldn't.

I dropped the matchbox and took a quick step back. Slapping my hands over my ears, I closed my eyes. I could control this. Despite the fact Ian was no longer here, I *could* control Laria and get rid of her once and for all.

And I wouldn't cut.

With a trembling hand, I picked up the matchbox and placed the razor blades back inside. I fell into the chair where Ian would always sit when he visited me, closed my eyes and wondered what he would do if he were here now. When I saw him that time after he'd passed over, he had told me to think of him and he would come. I was thinking of him now...and yet I didn't feel or sense him at all.

I tried to clear my thoughts and focus, control my breathing—basically all the things I'd read in the psychic How To books Miss A and her friend, Anne Marie had given me, but it was no use. I couldn't get the image of Laria standing in the schoolyard out of my head, no matter how hard I tried.

Ian please...Mom please...I need you guys.

It took a few minutes, but I started to feel a sense of comfort, which had to be my mom since I smelled vanilla, her favorite scent. I breathed in deep, savoring the smell, and the feeling of warmth and contentment that surrounded me.

Mom, I don't know what to do. Please help me.

I immediately calmed, feeling the panic wane by the second.

A strange sound alerted me that I wasn't alone. I opened my eyes, hoping maybe I had a sign from Ian or my mom. Scanning the room, I looked for the source of the scratching, and it took me a few seconds to realize where the noise came from. My headboard, where someone had carved the word DIF.

DIF?

The F slowly became an E.

DIE.

Chapter Two

I had just finished picking up the mess in my bedroom when Megan walked in without knocking. I bit back a scream.

"Sorry. I knocked but no one answered. I could hear Miss A singing in the kitchen when I walked up the stairs though." Megan's lips quirked. "If you ask me, that woman is tone deaf."

I laughed under my breath and fluffed the pillow, making sure the word DIE on my headboard wasn't visible.

"You know, we should have a sleepover here some night. I'd like to stay. But I'm telling you now that we will *not* be going down in the basement." She gave a shudder. "That place gives me the creeps."

The basement gave me the creeps, too, especially since Laria had attacked me there. I hadn't been down there since, and I had no plans to venture down there anytime soon. "You can sleep over whenever you want. Maybe Cassandra could come, too."

"Really?" she asked, checking herself out in the mirror on the back of my bathroom door. Megan was tiny—just a little over five feet tall. She weighed roughly a hundred pounds, and had the largest boobs I'd ever seen on a girl her size. Her shoulder-length auburn hair was a mass of curls and she had pretty brown eyes. "I'm glad you're warming to Cassandra. She's actually really sweet when you get to know her. Maybe a little too opinionated, but you'll get used to it."

I completely understood why Cassandra had an attitude with me when we'd first met. She liked Johan, and Johan had been interested in me when I first moved to Braemar. Emphasis on *had*. He'd been decent today at school, which was good. Since we ran in the same circles, it made sense to get along.

"Speaking of Cass, let's go," Megan said. "We have to pick her up."

"I thought she couldn't go out on school nights."

Megan's lips quirked. "She can't, but apparently she's going for it."

I grabbed my jacket out of the closet and followed her down the stairs and out the door.

Megan's car was still running, and before I opened the car door, I took a good look in the backseat to make sure no one was hiding back there.

What I wouldn't give to tell Megan about Laria, to have a confidante who knew what I was going through. Now that Ian was gone, she was my closest friend.

Or I could tell Miss Akin. After all, she was intuitive to a point... but I could see a certain fear in her eyes when I mentioned Laria before. Especially after the séance we'd had with Anne Marie—where Laria had scared the hell out of all of us. Miss A was the closest thing I had to a mom, and I didn't want her leaving...for any reason. And a malevolent spirit haunting the place you lived and worked was a pretty good reason to leave.

When Ian was still here, Anne Marie, a psychic herself, had seemed open to talking to me about Laria. Just yesterday Miss Akin had commented that Anne Marie wasn't even answering her calls anymore. If things got really desperate then I could talk to Shane. I knew he'd been affected by Laria before. He'd been having those strange dreams and feeling like someone was holding him down when he slept. The dreams had subsided after Ian had passed over, but would they continue again now that Laria had returned? I wondered.

Megan glanced at me. "So are you going to tell me about Kade?"

"He gave me a ride home, which took like two minutes from school to the inn."

"Seriously, that's all you have to say?" she asked, looking disappointed.

Kade MacKinnon intrigued me, and not just because he was Ian's descendant, but things he'd said made me believe he and Ian were the same person. That, and the physical similarities couldn't exactly be ignored. I didn't know a lot about reincarnation, but I was really curious if it was possible for a spirit to be earthbound and yet living at the same time. Maybe that's a question I could ask Anne Marie.

"Hey, text Cassandra real fast and tell her we're right around the corner."

I did as asked and immediately received a text back from Cassandra that read. *I'm headed toward the gates now. Park at the entrance!*

"She said to park at the entrance."

Megan turned onto a long, tree-lined road. I could make out an enormous grey stone manor house in the distance. Manicured lawns, fountains, and a large, wrought iron gate—it was incredible and looked more like a country club than someone's home.

"Wow, nice place," I said, hoping to get a look at the inside one day soon.

"Cass comes from old money. Her great-grandfather owned a shipping empire. This was just one of his many hunting lodges."

Hunting lodge, manor, house, whatever—the place was straight-up amazing.

"I can hardly wait until her birthday, which is coming up next month, by the way. She can do the driving then. She's been dropping hints to her dad about buying her a Beamer, but Cass said her step-mum has mentioned a few times how she'd like to get a Rolls Royce Phantom and retire her Mercedes."

"Poor Cassandra," I said.

Megan laughed. "I know. Would be nice, right?"

"Definitely." My dad had said when it came time for me and Shane to get cars, we'd have to buy our own...so I knew I wouldn't be driving for a while. When I did get my own car, it would be like Megan's—functional and economical.

"Oh my God, look at her," Megan said, nodding toward the gate, where Cassandra was squeezing through. She wore four-inch stilettos, skintight jeans and a black Lycra top with a plunging neckline. Her long platinum blonde hair was flatironed and her dark eye makeup was on the dramatic side.

Megan pulled closer, and hadn't even stopped before Cassandra opened the car door.

"Jesus, Cass...you could wait until I came to a complete stop."

Cassandra dove into the backseat, and looked over her shoulder at the house beyond the iron gate. "Bitchzilla told me I couldn't go. I snuck out the servants' entrance, but I think she's onto me." She buckled her seatbelt. Just then her phone rang. She glanced at it and hit *Ignore*. "Shit."

Megan's eyes widened. "Oh my God, she's headed this way."

A bone thin woman with dark brown hair and a fake tan ran down the driveway, her fake boobs bouncing with each step. She couldn't be a day over thirty, and she wore a hot pink velour sweat-suit that fit her like a second skin. "Cassandra!" she screamed.

"Floor it!" Cassandra yelled, and Megan didn't hesitate.

The glen was jammed full of cars, and I had butterflies in my stomach when I noticed Kade's Range Rover among them.

"Milo's not here yet," Megan said, searching the parking lot for her boyfriend's van. "Where the hell is he? He left before I did." She reached for her cell.

Cassandra rolled her eyes. "Um, he has his license now, so you're going to have to let go a bit. Plus, he has people to pick up just like you."

Megan ignored her and dialed his number. I could hear the head -banging music that was Milo's ringtone. She cussed under her breath when he didn't pick up and dropped the phone in her purse with a heavy sigh.

I grabbed my jacket, slid it on and followed behind Megan and Cassandra. Excitement rippled down my spine when I caught sight of Kade standing with Johan, Tom, and a group of girls I recognized from the schoolyard. The same girls who had been watching me talk to Kade earlier.

"You want a beer, Riley?" Cassandra asked, heading for the keg resting on the tailgate of an old station wagon.

I shook my head. "No thanks."

Cassandra lifted a brow. "Seriously?"

"I have homework I have to get done when I get home." It wasn't a lie. I had five pages to read for History, but I also had no desire to drink, because the last thing I needed was to get shit-faced, especially with Laria hanging around.

My gaze shifted across the clearing to where Joni was stepping out of a car with her older sister and a short, stocky guy with a shaved head who I had passed in the hallway earlier at school today.

I still hadn't seen Shane yet, and since he wasn't with Joni, I had to assume he was with Milo.

"There's Kade," Cassandra said, pointing toward the fire pit. "And big surprise—he's with Dana and her crew."

I could hear the sarcasm in Cassandra's voice.

Dana, the beautiful redhead was in my first period class, nonexistent skirt showing off her long, flawless legs and kick-ass body. The guys in the class were checking her out pretty hard. She wasn't as busty as Megan, but she came in a close second.

Figures.

Cait walked up to us and gave each of us a hug. Her jet black hair with chunks of platinum made her stand out in the crowd, and she wore a military looking charcoal shirt with pencil leg black pants and flats. "Took you guys long enough. I was beginning to think you might not show up."

"Did you come with your brother?" Cassandra asked, glancing at me and giving me a wink.

Subtle.

Cait smiled. "Actually, I did catch a ride with him. Sorry, thought I told you that."

Megan shrugged. "I kind of figured when you didn't call."

Something, or someone, beyond my shoulder caught Cassandra's gaze because her eyes widened and she immediately stepped behind me. "Bloody hell."

"What?" Megan asked, following her gaze. "Oh, you mean Tom?" She flashed a mocking grin. "I thought you liked him, Cass. At least that's what I heard."

"Bitch," Cassandra said under her breath. "I swear to God, I will never mix hard alcohol with Vicodin again."

Vicodin? I tried not to look too surprised, even though I was. I had no idea she'd popped pills that night at the glen.

"What a fuckin' mistake that was." She chewed on a fingernail. "He's been blowing my phone up ever since."

Megan snorted. "You must have been bloody outstanding for him to take on stalker status."

I didn't dare tell Cassandra that more than one person at school had asked me about her and Tom's hookup. I'd just shrugged and told them I knew nothing about it, thinking the two had just made out that night at the glen.

From Cassandra's reaction though, I had to think that maybe they'd done more than kiss.

"Shoot me now and put me out of my misery," Cassandra said, taking another swig off her pint. "Stage five clinger. Oh my God."

Cait's eyes widened. "Is that the Scotch from Bitchzilla's stash?"

Cassandra grinned and handed the pint to Cait. "Yep."

"I have to say, the woman might be psychotic, but she has great taste in alcohol," Cait said, before taking a swig.

"Finally!" Megan said, watching Milo pull up in a beat-to-shit circa-1970s van. The blue paint had faded in spots, and there was rust around the fenders. Somehow it fit him to a T. He came to a screeching halt six feet from a group of girls. The van backfired and the door opened a second later. Richie, Shane and two other guys poured out in a cloud of what I assumed to be pot smoke.

Chapter Three

I'm glad to see you made it," Kade said, and I glanced up, surprised he'd approached without me seeing him. He was gorgeous, wearing a long sleeved navy shirt that formed to his athletic body, and dark, low-riding jeans. The Celtic cross, just like mine, hung from his neck. "Hey," I said, my voice coming out a squeak.

Cassandra laughed under her breath and covered it with a cough.

It seemed like everyone was watching us.

"On the way here Johan and Tom told me about the night you were put in the mausoleum," Kade said, lowering his voice.

I'm sure Tom, who didn't seem to like me for some reason, enjoyed telling Kade every detail of my terrifying hour locked in the MacKinnon family mausoleum. "Yeah, that was quite the welcome."

"That wouldn't have happened if I'd been here." His blue eyes were intense as he watched me.

I believed him. "I survived."

The sides of his mouth lifted slightly. "It was brave of you to stick it out. I don't know many girls who would have stayed."

"I bet Cait would have."

"True," he said, grinning in full force now, and I wasn't ready for what that smile did to my insides. Once again I thought of Ian. It was difficult to separate the two. They were so much alike. Even their personalities seemed similar. Or was I just looking for those similarities?

He stared like he was studying my face. "I don't know what it is about you, but from the second I saw you, I felt like I'd seen you, or maybe even met you before."

My heart missed a beat. "Maybe I just have one of those faces."

"No." He shook his head. "No, it's not that. When I saw you, I experienced déjà vu. Have you ever felt that with someone?"

I nodded. "Yeah, I felt the same way when I met you." I said the words before I could stop myself.

His eyes brightened, and for a second his gaze shifted to my lips.

"Kade...you left me."

It was the chick with the big rack, her clique on her heels. The girls who had been giving me the dirty looks after school when I'd been talking to Kade.

Dana checked me out hard, her brows furrowed as though she couldn't quite figure out why a guy like Kade would be wasting his time talking to a girl like me. One of the girls glanced at my jeans, arched a penciled-in brow, and actually whispered in the ringleader's ear. Dana's glossy lips spread in a smug smile.

I felt like an insect under a microscope...and it didn't feel good.

"Kade, do you think you could give me a ride home? The girls have to leave early and I really want to stay." Dana's eyes widened a little, and I swear she blinked fast a few times. "Tom said it would probably be okay with you."

Oh my God, I seriously hated this bitch.

"Sure," Kade said, right before someone from behind me said my name. I glanced over my shoulder, but there was just Milo, Richie and some of his buddies talking.

I turned back around, and immediately heard my name again. Now it was being repeated in my ear, over and over again, making it impossible to concentrate on anything else. Except maybe for the way Dana stepped closer to Kade.

I saw Shane across the clearing, talking with Joni and some of her friends. My gaze shifted to the edge of the woods. Not twenty feet from where my brother stood, a man was watching us. He was tall, with brown, stringy hair, and dressed in old-fashioned clothing—a navy jacket, tight tan breeches, and white stockings and black buckled shoes. My insides twisted. Wasn't that the same man I'd seen at Braemar castle when I'd passed Ian over? The guy who had taken Laria by the hand and led her away?

Just then, I felt fingers splay on the very top of my head and begin to move downward, through my hair, over the nape of my neck, and down my back, stopping at the waistband of my jeans.

My insides twisted. I hoped someone I knew stood behind me—like a friend from school, but when I glanced over my shoulder, there was no one even close to me.

Terrified, I wondered if I should ask for a ride home and get out of here before things went from bad to worse.

The figure in the woods started fading.

Riley. My name was whispered in my ear. *Riley.* The last came in a growling tone that made the hair on the back of my neck stand on end.

In the trees, close to where the ghostly man had been, I saw a figure manifest, and my breath left me in a rush.

Oh my God...it was Ian.

Cruel laughter vibrated in my ears, confirming my thoughts. When I blinked, Ian, or the spirit masquerading as Ian, was gone.

My nails dug into my palms. I needed to leave now. How I wished I had my license.

Dana laughed at something her friend said, and suddenly I felt a burning ache spread across my left arm. Seconds later I experienced the sensation of nails raking across my back, gouging deep into my skin.

I glanced behind me and there was no one there. Rubbing my arm, I rolled up my sleeve and was shocked to see a large, red welt running down the length of my arm.

What the hell?

"What is that?" Dana asked, and everyone in the group, including Kade, looked at my arm.

The scratch was close to where I'd cut on my elbow—the scars' tiny, silvery lines that were too symmetrical to be anything but intentional cuts.

"Nothing," I said, pulling my sleeve back down, but Dana wouldn't have it.

"Let me see." She took a step toward me, grabbed my wrist and turned my arm to get a better look.

"Back off, Dana," Megan said in a not-so-nice tone.

I yanked my arm away.

Everyone turned to see what the commotion was about.

Dana's eyes narrowed. Maybe it was my imagination, but I swore she looked surprised and triumphant at the same time.

Had she seen the scars? I wondered. And if she had—would she say anything about it to Kade?

I was horrified to think that my new friends would learn my secret.

By the time Megan announced we had to leave, I was more than ready to go home. Kade had asked me a few questions, mostly about my classes and school, but we couldn't shake Dana who had listened intently to every word of our conversation.

Kade left, too...Dana on his heels.

I tried to ignore the jealousy I felt. It made no sense. I had only met Kade today, and yet I wanted to claw Dana's eyes out. I knew for a fact she felt the same way about me. I could feel her animosity from a mile away.

Cassandra let out a belch from the backseat and then immediately rolled down the window. "I shouldn't have had that last straight shot. I'm gonna blow chunks."

"Ew," Megan said, looking at Cassandra in the rearview mirror. "Lean out the window. I don't want to be scrubbing puke off my floor."

I noticed Cassandra had drank a lot more than usual tonight. Maybe because Tom kept watching her like a lost puppy. Obviously he liked her, but it was just as obvious that Cassandra didn't want anything to do with him after their last encounter.

"You okay?" Megan asked, looking concerned.

"Yeah, I'm just tired."

"I didn't notice those scratches on your arms earlier," she said barely above a whisper.

My heart sank to my toes. The last thing I needed was to explain scratches or cuts on my body. But I was caught, plain and simple. I'd put the jacket on at the glen, so she would have seen my arms before. "They were there. I got them yesterday. You know me—always running into something."

Cassandra made a horrible hurling sound from the backseat, followed by a splatter.

Megan groaned. "Tell me you had your head out the window."

"Thanks for your concern," Cassandra said under her breath. "Bitch." She collapsed on the backseat. "Oh…my…God, someone shoot me."

Megan pulled into Cassandra's driveway and braked hard. "Do you need me to walk you to the door?"

Cassandra popped up from the backseat and looked in the opposite direction of the house. She frowned, and then turned in the right direction. "Nah, I got it. Plus, Bitchzilla is probably waiting for me at the front door. God, I hate my life."

The iron gates opened.

"Yep, Bitchzilla is up. At least you won't have to walk up the driveway." Megan reached across me and opened the glove compartment. There was a tube of toothpaste, three packs of gum, and a roll of breath mints. She handed the mints to Cassandra. "Here, pop one—or three, before you go."

Cassandra promptly unrolled the silver wrapper and popped a few in her mouth.

"Thanks," she said around the mints.

Megan shifted the car into drive and drove up the driveway at a slow crawl.

"How do I look?" Cassandra asked, brushing a hand down her face.

She had mascara smeared under her eyes and a few chunks of puke in her hair. "Wipe under your eyes," I said, searching for a napkin or a tissue.

She used the hem of her shirt instead, flashing her lacy black bra.

"Nice," Megan said, trying hard not to laugh. When she stopped the car, she reached back and picked the chunks from Cassandra's hair. She tossed them out the window and then poured water from her bottle on her fingers.

Cassandra took a deep breath and released it. "Well, wish me luck."

"Good luck!" we said in unison.

The front door opened and the woman known as Bitchzilla stepped out, wearing a long, dark robe with a gold monogram P, arms crossed firmly over her chest.

We watched Cassandra weave her way up the brick pathway, toward the woman who didn't move a muscle.

"Poor Cassandra." Megan shook her head. "She's gonna feel like shit tomorrow."

I had no doubt of that. "Definitely."

Megan drove around the circular drive, out the iron gates that immediately shut behind us, and pulled back onto the main road. She glanced at me. "I had fun tonight."

"I did, too."

"Kade *really* likes you."

I couldn't help but grin. "I *really* like him, too."

She laughed under her breath. "I can tell. I'm happy for you, Ri. I am."

"Thanks."

"Oh, and just a word to the wise—watch out for Dana. That one's not used to losing."

"I'm not worried about Dana." Truth be told, I was more worried about what was waiting for me when I got home than my competition for Kade's affection.

"She dyes her hair, but tells everyone she's a natural redhead. Who is she kidding—we all saw her hair turn from auburn to a mousy brown when we were thirteen."

I noticed some hostility toward Dana, but I didn't bite. I was tired of talking about her. Plus, I could see the inn up ahead, lights shining in several of the upstairs rooms.

Chapter Four

Miss A was already in bed, and I was relieved. I wasn't in the mood to chat.

I went straight to my room where I immediately checked out the marks on my body. Four long, red welts covered my back and arms.

I was still shaken by what I saw at the glen. The cloaked figure, the man standing in the woods, and then what appeared to be Ian looking at me. But it wasn't Ian. I knew that.

Changing into pajamas, I cleaned my makeup off my face and sat on the edge of my bed. I opened the drawer in the nightstand and took out the drawing of Ian. What I wouldn't give to have that moment in time back. The way he had looked at me, the soft smile on his lips, the desire I had seen in his eyes.

I wouldn't lie—I ached for the times we'd had this summer, for the love I felt for him and the hole in my heart that would never be filled. Falling back on my bed, I breathed in deeply and remembered when we'd come so close to making love. The touch of those long-fingered hands on my body, and the feel of his hard body against mine.

I wanted to believe that Ian and Kade were one in the same, and yet I couldn't wrap my brain around the concept. I knew Ian said more than once that time on the other side wasn't the same as time was here...but what did that mean exactly, and could it be possible that Ian and Kade were the same person—the same soul?

And what about Kade repeating the words I had said to Ian not so long ago...or the feeling of déjà vu that Kade experienced when he'd first seen me. I pulled the books out from under my bed and scoured them for anything on reincarnation. They all basically said the same thing—that reincarnation was the soul being reborn into another body, that we went around and around again with the same group of people, learning new lessons with each incarnation.

I walked to the window and stared out at the castle, remembering the pull I had felt when I'd first seen it. There were lights on in nearly every room.

What was Kade doing now? I wondered. Was he thinking about me?

Suddenly, the castle became obstructed, and for a second I thought that the castle's power must have gone out. When I leaned closer to the window, I realized the obstruction was on my side. Strands of dark hair hid the castle from view.

A scream rose in my throat as I stared at Laria, who was upside down, and now watching me from the other side of the glass. Her dark eyes held a look of pure hatred, and her lips were curved in a sinister smile.

I yanked the drapes closed and ran for the door, only to find it locked tight.

Fear danced along my spine. How could it be locked from the hallway side?

I backed away from the door. I'd heard Shane come home

minutes after me, and immediately he'd turned on his music.

Freezing cold air enveloped me, along with a feeling of impending doom.

Slowly, I turned to face the malevolent spirit.

"You have no idea what I am capable of," Laria said, in a creepy disembodied voice.

"Shane!" I yelled.

I heard him lower the stereo volume.

"Shane!" I yelled again, and I heard something hit the floor and then his footsteps running toward me.

He tried the door, but it wouldn't budge. "Riley?"

I opened my mouth to respond, but Laria moved faster. Her hand clamped over my mouth.

"Open the door, Riley!" Shane said, the knob rattling as he tried to open the door.

"I'll kick it down if you don't open it in two seconds."

Laria released me abruptly and walked straight through the door.

The doorknob immediately stopped turning.

"Shane," I said, my heart hammering in my chest when I received no reply.

"Shane?" I tried the doorknob and it opened immediately.

Shane stood in the hallway, hands at his sides, frowning. "What the hell was that about?"

"Sorry, I freaked out when I couldn't open the door. I guess I just spooked myself."

"Why didn't you say anything when I was talking to you? For fuck's sake, you about gave me a heart attack."

It was on the tip of my tongue to tell him about Laria. I knew he'd felt her before and I wondered if he felt her around today. Then again, he was finally spending more time at home and the last thing he needed was to hear about a ghost who was haunting me.

His gaze shifted to my arm. "Where did the scratches come from?"

Did you scratch yourself? I could see the unspoken question in his eyes.

I shook my head. "I didn't do it."

He watched me for a second and nodded, but the way his gaze lingered on my arm made me wonder if he believed me. "Well, it's been a long night. I'll see you in the morning."

"Okay, goodnight." I shut the door and walked to my bed, furious at Laria and terrified at the same time. She had said I had no idea what she was capable of...and yet I had a horrible feeling I was about to find out.

I woke up to find Ian standing by my bed.

He was as beautiful as I remembered. Tall, broad-shouldered, amazing bone structure, and a face that brought women to their knees, myself included.

"You called me." His lips curved into a wide smile, showing those deep dimples that I loved. "I told you I'd be here whenever you needed me."

Relieved to see him, I reached out. He took my hand and lay down on the bed beside me. I melted into him. "I miss you so much."

His fingers slid through mine, his thumb brushing along the side of my index finger. "I'm right here, Riley. I'm always here."

I snuggled closer, closed my eyes and inhaled the woodsy, sandalwood scent of him. "I had the worst day today. Laria is back."

"She can only hurt you if you allow her to."

"I don't know what to do, Ian. She's so much stronger than I am."

"Shhh, do not worry." He kissed the top of my head. "I won't let anything happen to you."

I opened my eyes. I had forgotten how long his eyelashes were, or that heavy-lidded look that came into those beautiful blue eyes of his whenever he looked at me.

"You are smarter than she is, Riley."

I wasn't so sure about that.

He ran his fingers slowly up my spine, and I smiled. His touch felt like heaven.

With his other hand, he lifted my chin with gentle fingers and I stared into his brilliant blue eyes. He leaned in for a kiss. My eyes closed again. His lips were petal soft against mine. God, how I missed that kiss. How I missed this...just being with him, taking the comfort only he could give me.

"You cannot beat her," he said against my lips, but it wasn't his voice.

A bony hand curled around the back of my neck. My heart dropped to my toes, and I slowly opened my eyes to find Laria staring back at me.

Chapter Five

I woke in the morning feeling exhausted. Last night's dream had been more than a little unsettling. For that short time I had felt Ian with me, and it had been amazing...until I found myself staring into Laria's dark eyes.

Thank God when I did wake from that nightmare there had been no Laria in sight. I'd turned on the light in the bathroom, went back to bed and counted backward from a hundred.

Now, as I entered the school, I could only hope she would keep her distance.

"I need to talk to Milo before the bell rings," Megan said. "I'll meet up with you at lunch, okay?"

"Sounds good." I walked to my locker, opened it up, and took out my textbooks. Something fell and clattered on the floor by my feet.

Glancing down, I saw a razor blade.

Every muscle in my body tensed. Oh my God.

Someone had to have slid the blade through one of the locker's three vents. At first I wondered if it was Laria since she'd already taunted me with my matchbox full of razor blades. But something told me it had been someone living, specifically Dana who had questioned the scratches on my arm last night. Obviously she'd seen the old scars and put two and two together.

I glanced over my shoulder, and was relieved to see that no one was paying any attention. Picking up the blade, I closed my locker and that's when I saw Dana a few feet away, talking with friends... but all of them were looking at me.

"How's that *scratch* feeling today?" Dana said, loud enough for anyone within a thirty-yard radius to hear.

I opened my mouth, ready to respond when I heard *She's not worth it.*

It sounded like my mom's voice. Thank God. I needed her support more than ever right now. I took a deep breath and kept walking. I heard snickers come from Dana's direction. I scratched the back of my head using my middle finger.

Hearing gasps, I smiled.

I immediately went straight to the bathroom where I wrapped the razor blade in a paper towel and tossed it in the trash.

Unfortunately, I had forgotten Dana was in my first period class until I walked into the room. She wore a smug smile. My nails bit into my palms.

As the minutes ticked away, I tried to concentrate on what the teacher was saying, but I couldn't focus. I kept feeling a strange ripple, like someone was watching me. Someone not living.

I hoped for a visual of some kind, but nothing...

I did know that the spirit's energy didn't feel familiar to me.

No matter how hard I tried, I couldn't get anything else, so I assumed that maybe it was a spirit just passing through.

I did think back on something Anne Marie had told me once about being able to tap into people's thoughts. I tried it with the boy in front of me. As the teacher droned on, I focused my attention on the paper and clutched the pen in my hand.

I saw of all things, a puppy. A black mutt with white spots and round, ice blue eyes. Next I saw a Frisbee, and the boy in front of me throwing it at the dog, trying to teach it to fetch.

Toby.

I hadn't realized I said the name until the boy turned around. He was cute, with curly blonde hair and caramel-colored eyes. "What did you say?"

I swallowed hard. "Nothing."

"No, you said Toby. That's my dog's name."

I felt a myriad of emotions, mostly elation that I'd nailed it.

"Mr. Johnson, is there something you or Miss Williams would like to share with the rest of the class?" Mr. Monahan asked, staring at us from over the rim of his black-framed glasses.

The boy in front of me turned to face the front. "No, sir."

Snickers and laughter sounded throughout the room.

"Miss Williams?"

I shook my head. "No."

By the time class ended, I had tried head-tapping a few other students, including Dana. I got random information, like she was the baby of the family, pampered and never told "no" a day in her life. I received mostly fragmented thoughts, but I felt a sense of empowerment knowing that I could pick up certain information.

The bell rang and I stood. The boy in front of me turned. "Sorry, I didn't mean to get you in trouble."

"No worries," I said, tossing my notebook and pen into my backpack.

"My name is Aaron, by the way."

"Hey," I said. "I'm Riley."

"Ah, the American I've been hearing so much about."

My brows lifted.

"Nothing bad, I assure you," he said, laughing under his breath.

I was relieved to hear that. "That's good."

"What class do you have next?"

"Science."

"That would be in the three hundred block. I'm headed that way, too. I'll walk with you...if that's okay."

I gathered up my things, actually glad to have someone walk with me. "Sure."

He followed me out the door, and fell into step beside me.

"Again, I'm sorry about getting you in trouble. I thought you said Toby, my puppy's name."

"What kind of puppy is Toby?" I asked.

"He's a mix. Lab and Collie."

"Have you taught him to play fetch?" I asked before I could stop myself.

"Not yet."

My heart sank. Why had I seen the Frisbee?

"But I have high hopes that he'll pick up on it fast. I was playing Frisbee with friends the other day, and he kept chasing after it."

I could have hugged him. That small validation felt incredible and I grinned up at him. He looked a little surprised by my reaction, but he grinned back at me.

I glanced up the steps and saw Kade coming toward us. Seeing me, he smiled. "Hey you," he said, his gaze shifting to Aaron before settling back on me again.

"Hi Kade."

The crowd moved us along, not giving either one of us a chance to stand and chat. "See you at lunch?" he said.

"Sure," I replied.

Aaron didn't miss a beat. He kept talking, and all I had to do was nod. I got that he was an only child to older parents who expected a lot out of him.

When we got to my next class, he opened the door for me.

I could hear a few snickers.

The warning bell sounded. "Thanks," I said.

"See you around," he said.

Cait was sitting in the back row. "What's with you and violin boy?"

I frowned. "Violin boy?"

"Aaron is a prodigy. He wrote his first song when he was like seven years old."

I was impressed. I'd never met a prodigy before.

"Well, what gives?" she asked, brows lifted high.

"Nothing. He walked me to class, that's all."

"How sweet," she muttered under her breath.

The bell rang and I took my seat in the second row. The teacher's accent was so thick I had a tough time understanding her. She had a habit of walking up and down the rows, her way of making sure we were all paying attention.

"Open your textbooks to page 309," the teacher said from behind me.

I flipped open my book to page 309 and my heart skipped a beat.

The razor blade.

How was that even possible? I'd just thrown it away.

Footsteps sounded beside me. I slammed the book shut and reached for my backpack.

"Forget something, Miss Williams?"

"Pencil," I said, feeling my cheeks turn hot as everyone stared.

I didn't want to think what would happen if she saw the razor blade.

Thankfully, she continued to walk past me, and asked a boy in the first row to start reading the text.

I kept my left hand over the razor blade while I wrote notes with the other. When the class flipped the pages, I did the same and finally relaxed.

Twenty minutes into class, I felt the familiar sensation of once again being watched. Staring at the paper on my desk, I focused. The good news was, the spirit didn't have a heavy or dark feel to it.

Feeling brave, I mentally asked the spirit to come closer.

I decided the presence felt male. I got an image of kids playing ball outside in the schoolyard, but oddly the picture was in black and white, and the clothes went back generations. Interesting. I wrote down what I was seeing and tried to push the spirit for more.

From the corner of my eye I saw something, or someone, move. They moved so fast though, that by the time I turned to look, there was nothing there.

Chapter Six

I met my friends at lunch.

My back was to the doors leading into the cafeteria, but I knew when Kade walked in because Megan glanced past my shoulder, then looked at me and grinned.

I didn't glance back, even though I wanted to.

"Is this seat taken?" Kade asked, motioning to the spot beside me.

My heart gave a little skip. "No, go ahead."

He slid in beside me, and sat so close our thighs touched. I noticed he always had a slightly disheveled look about his hair—like he was constantly running his fingers through the dark strands. "Did you have fun last night?" he asked, twisting the top off his juice and taking a drink.

"I did. What about you?"

"I had a great time...except for one thing."

I reached for my spoon, almost dreading his answer. "What thing?"

One side of his mouth lifted. "I didn't get your mobile number."

I released the breath I hadn't realized I'd been holding. It was tough to play it cool when I was so elated. Kade MacKinnon was asking for my cell number. "I'll give you my number…if I can get yours?" I was surprised I'd said that, but glad I had when his eyes lit up.

While we were exchanging phone numbers, Johan joined us, followed by Tom. The minute he sat down Cassandra bailed, saying she had to go to the library to get a research paper done.

Tom watched her leave, and although he'd been a dick to me since I'd met him, I actually felt sorry for him. He had it bad for her, and Cassandra obviously didn't feel the same.

"Are you coming to the game on Friday?" Kade asked, his voice sounding hopeful.

"I plan on it." It had been a while since I'd seen Shane play, and I wasn't going to miss it. Plus, any excuse to see Kade was a good enough reason to go.

He lifted his hand and brushed at my lips with his index finger. "You have a crumb there."

His touch was electric, sending a current through my entire body.

He dropped his hand to his side. We fell into silence for a few minutes, and I wished we'd have some time alone.

"So Kade, are you going to Milo's party this weekend?" Megan asked, spearing a peach with a plastic fork.

"Definitely. What time?"

"Eight or nine. His band is playing at ten, so make sure you're there by then."

"I wouldn't miss it. Thanks." He glanced at me. "You'll be there, right?"

I was encouraged that he had asked me first about the game and now about Milo's party. "I'll be there."

I remembered the last party at Milo's—how Laria had been there, terrorizing me, touching Shane, and how Ian had saved the day. I no longer had Ian, but I did have a friend in Kade. I felt comforted by him, the familiarity whenever we were together, and I also had my friends. They would be there for me. I knew it.

After school, I had Megan drop me off at the end of Anne Marie's driveway.

There was a newspaper in the middle of the gravel drive, and as I picked it up, I could hear Diggs, Anne Marie's dog, barking.

I walked up the steps and knocked on the door. To the right, the steel mailbox was crammed full of mail.

My stomach tightened in a knot. I didn't know Anne Marie all that well, but what I did know about her, she didn't come across as the kind to let her mailbox overflow...or ignore phone calls from her friends.

Miss Akin hadn't mentioned anything about Anne Marie leaving town. Plus, she'd never leave Diggs.

I rang the doorbell and heard barking again.

At first there was nothing but silence, and then I heard movement in the house. I waited for a minute, then another, surprised when she didn't answer.

I rang the doorbell again and finally looked through the front window. Nothing seemed out of place. The small living room appeared just as I remembered it—cluttered and lived in, even down to the teacup sitting on the side table next to the rocker Anne Marie had sat in when I'd last visited her.

Maybe she was just taking a nap, I thought to myself. But wouldn't she wake up to the doorbell and to Digg's barking?

In my peripheral vision I saw what looked like someone standing in the entryway near the front door but in the shadows. The hair on the back of my neck stood on end. It could be Anne Marie, but why would she hide and not say anything?

"Anne Marie, it's me—Riley."

I felt a sudden pressure in my chest, and had the unmistakable feeling that something was very wrong. Maybe the person hiding wasn't Anne Marie at all. What if it was a robber...or a spirit?

A part of me wanted to break down the door, and the other wanted to run and never look back.

"Can I help you?"

I gasped and whipped around to find a man wearing coveralls standing on the first step. He had a crowbar clenched tight in his fist.

"Um—I'm looking for Anne Marie."

"She's gone to visit her daughter."

"She left Diggs?"

"Of course not," he said, looking at me like I was crazy to even suggest such a thing. "She'd never leave Diggs behind. That dog is like one of her kids."

"Maybe I was just hearing things."

"Could be you were hearing one of my mutts." He pointed to an old stone cottage that was barely visible through the trees. "I have five."

That would explain the barking...if it hadn't have sounded like it was coming from inside the house. I was tempted to mention the figure standing in the entry, but decided against it.

"She'll be returning on the twenty-sixth."

Damn, the twenty-sixth was weeks away.

I heard a bark from inside the house again. Apparently the man heard it, too, because he frowned, his gaze shifting from me to the door and back again. "I've got a key in case of emergencies."

He pulled out a key chain with about twenty odd keys on it. After three tries, he finally found the right one and the door opened.

"Anne Marie?" he called cautiously. "Anne Marie, are you here? Diggs?"

Nothing. No bark, no scuffle, nothing.

In the kitchen there was a partially full teacup on the counter, and a spoon sitting beside a fly-covered scone. In the sink there were pots, pans and dirty dishes.

Anne Marie's house had been tidy the last time I'd been here. If she had known she was leaving for a while, then why hadn't she taken the time to at least wash her dishes?

It seemed out of character. The man cracked open a window and swatted at the flies. I walked down the hallway, past a bedroom set up as an office, a bathroom with pink tiles, and the master bedroom...where the bed was unmade.

Okay, now I was really getting nervous.

"When did you say she left?" I asked, heading back to the kitchen.

"Few days ago," he said, pulling off his hat and scratching his bald head. "I saw her walk to her car with a suitcase and Diggs. Normally she'll tell me ahead of time if she's going somewhere, so I was surprised she hadn't said anything to me."

"Miss Akin, our housekeeper, said Anne Marie hasn't been feeling well."

His eyes lit up. "You're the American girl who lives at the inn?"

"That would be me."

"Anne Marie mentioned you once or twice." He checked the

garbage under the sink, pulled the liner out and tied the top. "I've heard stories of that place."

Even the way he said "that place" sounded ominous. "What kind of stories?"

It seemed most every place in Braemar was haunted, even Anne Marie's. A shiver rushed up my spine.

He shrugged. "You know…all old buildings have stories."

My cell rang, signaling that I had a text. "Speak of the devil—it's Miss Akin," I told him. "It's time for me to get home."

The old man shifted on his feet. "Will you tell her Harry said hello?" I swore his cheeks turned pink.

"Sure," I said, walking toward the front door. "Harry, will you let me know if you hear anything from Anne Marie?"

"Aye, lass, I certainly will."

I pulled out Laria's journal from between my mattress. I had read the spell that had bound Ian to the land so many times when Ian had still been here, I could probably recite it word for word. Regardless, I read it again, aloud, and wondered where I had gone wrong.

I fished under my bed for the other books on witchcraft and spent the next hour trying to find out what I could about breaking spells. It was tough—because spells were specific to the person creating it.

Then it dawned on me—what if Laria's return didn't have to do with the curse at all? What if it was me she wanted revenge on now that Ian was gone?

Miss Akin called me down for dinner. She had been quiet since I'd told her that Anne Marie had left for her daughter's house. I couldn't help but feel partly responsible for the drama happening in Anne Marie's life. After all, she'd started acting weird after the séance where Laria had made her appearance. She'd told me herself when I'd visited her last that Laria was visiting her on a daily basis, and even invading her dreams.

Shane came down to dinner after being called for the third time. The back of his hair stood up straight, so I took it he'd been sleeping. Miss Akin asked him about practice and he just shrugged.

She cleared her throat. "Coach Everson called and said you were in a fight."

I turned to Shane. "With who?"

He took a deep breath, released it. "Calvin Eckhart. Trust me, he had it coming. He's a prick."

"Shane," Miss A said, looking like he'd slapped her. "Watch your mouth or I will wash it out with soap."

"Sorry," he replied, cutting his spaghetti with his fork. "A person can only take so much sh—crap before they snap. He's always running his mouth."

Calvin Eckhart? The name didn't ring a bell.

"He was sent home too," he said, like that made all the difference.

Miss Akin sighed heavily. "Your dad wouldn't—"

"He called Joni a few choice names and I didn't like it. When he didn't stop, I clocked him."

At least he'd gotten in trouble sticking up for Joni.

He set his fork down. "Please don't tell Dad about it. We were just sent home early from practice. I mean, we weren't suspended or anything."

"Speaking of Dad—did he call?" I asked Miss Akin, intent on changing the discussion.

"Not yet."

"He's seeing a woman," Shane said matter-of-factly. "Why else would he be spending so much time away from home?"

"No, he's not." The very thought of Dad dating horrified me.

"Let's not start speculating," Miss Akin said, looking uncomfortable. "I'm sure your father would tell you if he was seeing someone."

Shane snorted and lifted the glass of milk to his lips.

I thought back over the weeks since we'd been in Braemar and how Dad had almost immediately set out for Edinburgh. I know his company headquarters was there, but the reason he'd bought the inn, or so he'd said, was so he could work from home in peace and quiet. But that had been when we'd still lived in Portland.

I couldn't help but wonder if Shane was right. If Dad had a girlfriend, I don't know what I'd do. I ran a hand through my hair. As if I already didn't have enough to worry about.

Chapter Seven

The following day in first period I felt the familiar sensation of being watched. When the teacher gave us time to read for the better part of the hour, I instead focused on spirits.

Minutes in, I heard a sigh come from behind me.

I straightened my spine. I didn't know if it was another student, or if I was hearing a ghost. I figured the latter when cold air worked its way up my legs.

"You're the girl who helped Ian."

I glanced to my right. Ronald Delano, a boy with flatironed hair, rolled his pencil between his thumb and forefinger while he read the textbook. Sensing my gaze, he looked at me, or rather my boobs, and blushed before he turned his attention back to his book.

"Over here, by the map."

I glanced toward the map and saw a boy with short, sandy blonde hair sitting on a table where all the research books were kept. Dressed in dark shorts, suspenders and a white shirt, it was obvious he wasn't from my time.

"What are you doing?" he asked me telepathically.

"Um, what are you *doing?"* I thought.

He slipped off the desk and walked past the teacher, touching the edge of each as he approached me.

"I'm talking to you."

Little smart-ass. *"What's your name?"* I asked, elation racing through me. I was talking to a spirit—a benevolent spirit from what I could tell.

"Peter."

"Is this where you live?"

"More or less."

Was he trying to be evasive?

"How long have you been dead?"

He glanced at the calendar on the wall and pursed his lips together. *"Ninety-two years, four months, six days...in your time."*

There it was again—that mention of time. *"In my time. What does that mean exactly?"* I asked, curious for an explanation.

"You think of time as being in a straight line with a beginning, a middle, and an end."

"It's not?"

He laughed, or actually giggled, the sound making me smile. *"No, time is an illusion."*

I wished he'd expand on the time explanation a bit, but he didn't. Instead, he acted like a typical ten-or-so-year-old boy and flicked Ronald's textbook.

Ronald frowned, shot me a strange look, and I pretended to be interested in what I was reading.

"Actually, I'm eleven."

"Hey, I was close. I'm curious...how come you didn't move on? I mean, why stay here?"

He fidgeted, pulling the zipper on my backpack. *"I didn't want to leave my family."*

Given how long he'd been earthbound, I had to believe all of his family had all passed on by now. At least those he had known in his lifetime. *"What do you do to pass the time?"*

He shrugged. *"Lots of things. That's why I like school so much. There is so much to see and do. Plus, I like driving the teachers a bit mad. Moving objects here and there. Mrs. Abernathy gets especially freaked out, probably because she is sensitive...like you."*

My pulse leapt. Mrs. Abernathy, the art teacher, was a sensitive?

Throughout Science, Peter stayed close by, and even served as comic relief. He rattled off the answers to the questions of a surprise quiz. I felt a little guilty when I got one hundred percent right, but who was I to look a gift horse in the mouth? I even caught him staring at Cait a few times. I suspected he had a little crush.

In Mrs. Abernathy's art class, I watched her closely. Whenever Peter would step near her, she would tilt her head to the side and lose her concentration.

Peter flashed a cocky smile. *"Told you."*

At lunch, Peter sat at my table—literally on the table—his legs kicking back and forth. I was reminded of the days when Ian was around, how I had to pretend he didn't exist when I was with other people. It was tough to ignore him.

When Cait showed up wearing a red baby doll dress with white polka dots, and black leggings, Peter grinned, his gaze slowly shifting over her long, thin legs. Cait received a few whistles as she made her way toward our table, and in true Cait fashion, she ignored them.

"Hey, you want to come over and work on our science assignment tonight?" Cait asked.

I won't lie—I was excited and yet nervous at the prospect of being in the castle again. "Sure."

I could feel Megan watching us, and when I glanced at her, she smiled softly. I think she was the only one who realized how much I liked Kade. Maybe Cassandra and Cait did, too, but I told myself it wasn't because of Kade that I was excited about going to the castle. And yet, when Kade walked into the cafeteria a few minutes later wearing a black T-shirt and dark jeans, I called myself a liar. He was gorgeous and I had a tough time concentrating on anyone else. Even the eleven-year-old ghost who was snickering at me.

"How about four o'clock?" Cait said.

I knew for a fact that Shane had football practice until five, so chances that I would actually run into Kade were pretty good. It just depended on if he was coming home right after practice.

Kade looked in my direction. I could feel his gaze from across the cafeteria and I forced myself to not look at him. I had been so obvious up to now, and I just wanted to play it as cool as I could. So when he sat down at a table with his friends, I was disappointed. I'd hoped he would sit by me again.

"You are not foolin' anyone, Riley."

I glanced at Peter, who shook his head. *"That one over there is sweet on you as well."*

He motioned toward the table to my right. Aaron sat with a small group of boys and girls. His friend nudged him and he glanced over my way. He waved, and I waved back. Cait followed my gaze. "I wouldn't do that if I were you. You're going to give the boy hope."

"He's a friend," I said in defense, dropping my gaze to my plate. I definitely didn't want to be sending out any mixed signals. Been there, done that with Johan.

Peter snorted and took a seat beside Cait. She didn't show any sign that she noticed his presence.

"Oh hey, Megan...I forgot to tell you that Sheila said Milo's band sounds like shit."

Megan's face dropped. "What the hell does she know what Milo's band sounds like?"

Cassandra shrugged and took a bite of salad. "That's exactly what I asked her. She said she heard he sucked."

"Bitch," Megan said. "He's bloody brilliant. You just wait and see."

"I've heard him. I know how good he is," Cassandra said, cracking open a diet soda.

"He is good," Cait added. "Damn good."

Megan immediately relaxed. "Thanks guys."

"I'm excited to hear him play," I said, meaning it. I couldn't wait for Milo's party.

Chapter Eight

I was tense as I knocked on the front door of Braemar castle. Despite the fact Kade was at practice, which was a relief in itself, I had to be sure not to say anything or let on that this wasn't my first visit to their home. It's not like I'd blurt out, "Hey, I'm the one who broke into your home while you were on holiday to perform a ritual to free your ancestor Ian from a curse put on him by a dead, but very evil witch." Yeah, that'd go over *so* well.

I glanced over my shoulder and Peter waved at me from where he sat on the stone wall—the same stone wall I had originally seen Laria. He hadn't wanted to come closer to the castle, and, in a way, I was relieved. I definitely didn't need him distracting me.

The door opened and a petite, cute woman with soft brown eyes and auburn hair cut in a bob smiled back at me. She wore yoga pants, a Nike T-shirt and blinding white tennies. "You must be Riley Williams," she said, extending a hand. "It's so lovely to meet you. I am Karen, Cait's mum."

Honestly, I didn't see any resemblance between Cait, Kade, and their mom. I suppose I was expecting someone who looked like Maggie, Ian's mum, with dark hair and large blue eyes to open the door. I shook her hand, and her grip was surprisingly strong.

"It's nice to meet you, too."

Her grin widened. "I like your accent."

I had grown used to hearing those words, especially since school had started. Funny, but I had never thought of myself as having an accent.

"Hey," Cait said, coming around the bend in the stairs.

"Hey."

"Would you like anything to drink, Riley?" Karen asked. "A cup of tea, perhaps?"

"No, I'm fine, thanks."

Cait rolled her eyes and took me by the hand. "Come on. Mum, we'll be in my room."

"Dinner is at six. Would you like to stay, Riley?"

Staying for dinner meant I'd see Kade. "Sure, that would be great," I said before I could talk myself out of it.

"Great. Would you like me to call your parents?"

"No, I'll let Miss Akin know."

Her brow furrowed slightly, but she nodded. "Very well."

Cait motioned for me to follow her.

I had to admit, I felt guilty for having broken into their home as we rounded the turret steps. We passed by a few doors, and then stepped into a room that was a glaring scarlet red. The curtains were black and there were crosses and angels everywhere...but I liked it. "Nice," I said, tossing my backpack on her bed. There was a little cubbyhole room, and she had her laptop setting on a desk in the small space.

"My mum freaked when I picked out the color, but she's warming to it...or so she says. She told me she's glad she doesn't have to sleep in here."

That sounded like something my mom would have said. I saw a board with pictures of friends. Cait had used safety pins to hang the pictures. I smiled seeing Megan in a lot of the photos, and I recognized the glen in more than one shot. My pulse skittered seeing Kade, sans shirt, playing football. He had an incredible body—nice wide chest, perfect pecs, a solid six-pack and the deep V that disappeared beneath the waistband of his pants. The same deep V that made girls get stupid, myself included.

It took effort, but I pulled my gaze away from the photo and dialed Miss Akin before I forgot. She told me to have a good time and to please get a ride home so I didn't walk home in the dark. I agreed with her. No way would I be walking home with Laria on the loose.

"We should probably get our homework done," I said, dumping my books out on the black comforter.

Cait sighed and opened her textbook. Although she spent a lot of time talking in class, I could tell she'd paid attention to at least some of what our teacher had said. We flew through the homework and talked for a while. We actually liked a lot of the same bands and movies. I asked her about boys and she didn't seem too interested in any one guy, except for maybe Shane.

I heard the front door open and close, and footsteps coming up the stairs. My heart pounded in time with the steps...that stopped shy of Cait's bedroom.

Excitement raced up my spine. Kade was home.

Fifteen minutes later Cait's mom knocked on the door. "Girls, dinner is ready."

"We'll be right there," Cait replied. "My mum is downright anal when it comes to hand washing. Go ahead," she said, nodding toward the bathroom.

The bathroom was a strange shape, not surprising given the fact it was in a castle tower. I wish I'd brought my backpack in with me. I'd just have to slip some lip gloss on when Cait washed her hands. I finger-combed my hair, and leaned forward to make sure I had no eye boogers. My breath caught in my lungs. In the mirror's reflection I saw a tall, massive man with long red hair, a scruffy beard and dirt on his cheeks. I opened my mouth to yell for Cait when the man disappeared.

"You coming?" Cait called from the other side of the door.

"Jesus," I said under my breath, placing a hand over my pounding heart. I needed to calm down.

Cait and I walked into the dining room and I smiled seeing the picture of Maggie, Ian's mom, hanging above the fireplace. Maggie had been the reason I had found Laria's journal in the first place, not to mention she'd given me comfort when I'd been locked in the mausoleum while Laria had been tormenting me. Seeing her brought those memories back.

"Ah, this must be Miss Williams who I have heard so much about. It's lovely to have you in our community," said a man who sat at the end of the long table reading a newspaper. He had the MacKinnon look about him—dark hair, which had gone gray at the temples, and the same brilliant blue eyes as Kade and Cait's.

"Riley, this is my dad," Cait said.

"Thank you for having me, Mr. MacKinnon."

"Please, call me Duncan."

Duncan. The same name as Ian's brother. "Thank you, Duncan."

"My wife has made some traditional Scottish fare tonight, and I'll be interested to see how it compares to your American cuisine."

"Her housekeeper is Scottish, Dad," Cait said. "So it's not like she hasn't been eating traditional Scottish food. Isn't that right, Riley?"

"Well, we have the finest beef on the menu," he said before I could respond to Cait. "You're not one of those vegetarians, are you?"

"Nope," I replied. "I'm a meat and potatoes girl all the way."

"Thank goodness for that," he said with a wink.

I smiled and took the seat beside Cait. A girl about twelve years old walked in and stopped when she saw me, eyes narrowing as she checked me out. She dressed like a mini Cait with ripped stockings under purple shorts, and suspenders over a black tank top. There any similarity ended. The girl was slightly chunky, had strawberry blonde hair, silver eyes, and wore a pair of wire frame glasses. Seeing me check her out, she lifted a brow.

"This is Madison," Duncan said.

"Hey Madison," I said, shifting under her intense stare. "I didn't realize Cait had a little sister."

Madison scowled. "Uh, maybe because I'm her cousin, dipshit."

"Madison!" Duncan said, shaking his head. "Apologize to Riley right now."

"Sorry," she said, taking a breath and sliding into the chair directly across from me.

Karen walked into the room and began filling everyone's glasses with ice water. "Maddy has been living with us for a little over a year now, isn't that right?"

"I'll spare you and my aunt any awkwardness by spilling my bio," Madison said glumly. "My mum is a druggie and I have no idea who my dad is, so lucky Aunt Karen and Uncle Duncan get to take care of me until Mum gets her act together, which might be this decade, but it's doubtful."

The girl was to the point; I'd give her that. For all her 'I-don't-give-a-crap-attitude', I sensed she was a little lost.

"We love having you with us, Madison," Karen said, a bit too quickly. "And I know that sister of mine will make it through rehab this time."

Madison rolled her eyes and slumped in the chair.

Not that I was happy about Madison's less than happy life, but it was nice to know that the MacKinnons had their own share of drama in their family. It made me feel a little less self-conscious about my dysfunctional home life.

Karen walked toward the door where she called out, "Kade, come to the table please."

My heart pounded hard as I heard his footsteps draw nearer. I felt kind of stupid for being here, which was ridiculous, I told myself. After all, Cait had invited me over to study, and it was their mom who had asked me to dinner. I wasn't stalking him or anything.

Kade walked in the room, wet hair curling at the collar of a soft grey T-shirt that formed to his perfect body. Well-worn jeans completed the outfit and he was actually barefoot. S-E-X-Y.

His gaze immediately shifted to me. "Riley," he said, his voice mirroring the surprise on his face. "I didn't know you were here."

"Homework with Cait," I said, reaching for my glass. My hand was trembling, and from the corner of my eye I could see Madison watching me closely.

Kade's soft smile immediately put me at ease, and he surprised me when he sat at the far end of the table, closest to me. He unfolded his napkin and laid it in his lap. "I'm glad you're here."

"Oh my God, barf," Madison said under her breath, and Kade completely ignored her. I had a tougher time ignoring her, especially since she sat directly across from me.

I returned Kade's smile. "Thanks. I am, too."

Madison coughed and said "sick" at the same time.

"Knock it off, Maddy," Cait said between clenched teeth.

Karen took the seat to her husband's right, and I was glad the parents were at the opposite end of the table. I would rather be sitting across from a smart-ass twelve-year-old than Duncan and Karen.

Duncan clapped his hands together. "Well, if we're ready. Let's pray."

We hadn't prayed at my house since before my mom died.

Cait took my right hand and Kade my left. I barely even heard the prayer, especially when Kade's long fingers tightened around mine. I resisted the urge to glance at him, even though I could swear I felt him watching me. Sure enough, when the prayer ended and I opened my eyes, he was looking at me with a soft smile.

My mouth watered as a steak garnished with grilled mushrooms was set before me with sides of small potatoes and green beans. It was impossible not to be self-conscious as I ate, since everyone watched me expectantly. "The steak cuts like butter," I said, surprised at how tender the meat was and how easy it was to cut. I added, "So good," for extra effect.

Karen beamed.

"So…tell us what it's like to be an American living in rural Scotland," Duncan said, lifting a glass of wine to his lips.

I wiped my mouth with my napkin and sat up straighter. "Well, it's different, that's for sure."

Madison snorted and said something unintelligible under her breath.

Cait frowned at her. "Um, have you ever been to America, Maddy?"

Madison's eyes widened and she shook her head.

"Exactly, so shut up."

Karen sighed heavily. "Girls, stop it. Our guest doesn't want to hear your bickering, nor do I for that matter."

Cait clenched her jaw. "Then maybe she shouldn't be the peanut gallery whenever I have someone over."

Madison looked down at her plate. I felt sorry for her—this girl who had been discarded by both parents. She had an attitude, and I could understand why. Maybe underneath the tough façade there was a sweet girl trying to deal with the fact she'd been abandoned.

Karen poured a cup of tea. "So I understand your father is a computer programmer or something like that."

I nodded. "That's right."

"And your mother?"

I was surprised she didn't know about my mom. Then again, I had to remember they had all just returned from vacation and probably hadn't heard the local gossip. "My mom died last year."

Madison looked up at me, and then glanced at Karen, who set her fork down.

"I'm—I am so sorry, Riley. I didn't know..."

"It's okay," I said, surprised at how calm I felt when talking about my mom now. I felt a certain amount of peace about her death. After crossing Ian over, she had visited me and told me I hadn't been responsible for her death. Essentially, it had been her time to go.

"Was it an illness?" Karen asked. Beside me, Kade had stopped eating.

"A car wreck," Madison said, and everyone looked at her.

Chapter Nine

Madison's eyes were the size of saucers...as though she couldn't believe she'd said the words aloud.

"That's right," I said, curious she had known the specifics. Maybe she'd overheard Cait talking, but even Cait seemed surprised.

Or was Madison like me and she could head-tap?

I wanted to ask her how she knew, but I didn't want to put her on the spot, especially since Cait already looked like she wanted to choke her.

Madison glanced past my shoulder and then quickly looked down at her plate.

The table went quiet.

I cut the steak into bite-sized pieces, and was almost grateful when Duncan asked, "So it's just you and your father?"

"And my brother. He's a year younger. Actually, we're only ten months apart. We nearly ended up in the same grade," I said with a smile, and everyone at the table seemed to relax.

"What a nightmare that would be," Cait said under her breath.

"Ah, come on, sis...it wouldn't be so bad." Kade's voice was teasing. "Actually, no, you're right. It would be a nightmare."

Everyone laughed, including Madison, which eased the tension.

"A sad tale, lass."

I turned toward the sound of the male voice, and the hair on my arms stood on end. Beside the fireplace, arms crossed over his massive chest, was the man I had seen in the bathroom. He wore a tunic and a kilt, both of which were a bit ragged.

Everyone at the table had followed the direction of my stare. Oh my God—I was so busted. "That's a beautiful picture," I said, nodding toward the portrait of Maggie. Do you know who it is?"

Karen grinned. "That is our ancestor, Lady Maggie MacKinnon. I love her kind face and soulful eyes. She's just so striking, isn't she?"

"Yes, she is," I agreed. And what a beautiful spirit she was.

"You should have seen her in person. What a lovely lass," the spirit said, falling into a sprawl in one of the two plush chairs that sat in front of the fireplace. "I have never met her equal in all my years."

I pulled my gaze away from the giant. Madison's brows furrowed as she looked from me, then in the direction of the chair where the spirit sat.

"Maggie loved to paint. In fact, I have some portraits she painted of her family—"

"Oh my God, Mum...really?" Cait said, brows lifted nearly to her hairline.

"Actually, I would love to see them," I blurted, excited to see them. "I was reading a book about the town and I came across information about the family."

Duncan set his fork down. "Have you now?"

I nodded. Oh crap. Maybe I shouldn't have said that. "Miss Akin knows a lot about the history of Braemar, and let's face it—the castle is at the heart of the history." I picked up the glass, took a long drink, and hoped they didn't think I was strange.

"More like you loved the MacKinnon boy, lass," the spirit said.

"Seriously, Ri...don't get her started," Cait said under her breath.

"I draw a little myself, so I'd love to see them," I said, anxious to turn the attention away from me.

Karen clapped her hands together. "Lovely, a fellow artist."

Cait shook her head.

Under the table I felt toes nudge my foot.

I glanced at Kade. He lifted his glass and took a drink of milk, watching me over the rim all the while. I wondered if he was playing footsie with me because he wanted me to not encourage his mom... or because he was flirting.

"You're a spry one, aren't you, lass?"

There was the giant again.

I didn't turn and look at the spirit, but I caught Madison's gaze on me. Was it my imagination or was she looking from me to where the giant sat?

"I'll be right back," Karen said, jumping up from the table.

"Great," Cait said, sounding irritated. "She's a fanatic when it comes to art."

Kade's foot brushed along my ankle, then up my calf.

I liked what he was doing—loved his touch, and the way it made me feel all fluttery inside.

Duncan poured himself another glass of wine. "I'd like to have your family over for dinner one night."

It took me a second to realize Duncan was speaking to me, and I felt my face turn warm. "My dad is in Edinburgh right now, but I'm sure he'd love to meet you," I said, my voice husky sounding.

The giant snickered.

I had to stop myself from turning around and telling him to be quiet. Instead, I took another bite of steak and chewed the piece at least twenty times.

Duncan nodded. "Let's schedule something soon."

Karen walked in carrying a plastic storage box.

Cait's mouth opened. "Bloody hell, Mum..."

"Come, Riley," Karen said, motioning toward the two chairs. "Sit with me."

I set my napkin on the table, flashed Kade a smile, and walked over to the chairs.

Karen sat in one chair, and I wasn't about to sit on the giant, so I sat cross-legged on the floor.

"You can sit in the other chair," Karen said.

"That's okay. I like being closer to the fire. I'm a little cold." A total lie, since I'd broken into a sweat when Kade started playing footsie with me.

"These are all of the Braemar countryside," Karen said, unrolling one of many paintings.

Maggie had been a talented artist, just like Ian had mentioned. "I like her muted tones," I said, and it was odd because touching her work, I could see images in my mind. Maggie painting—the way she had set up her easel, the little folding chair she took with her, how she prepared the paints as the breeze lifted her hair while she painted the landscape before her. And she always wore a cream-colored straw hat with a pink ribbon every single time she painted. Oddly I knew that bit of information with a certainty that surprised even me.

"Here is her family."

My heart instantly flew to my throat. Ian must have been all of ten, and his siblings younger. Even as a boy, there were signs of the handsome man he would one day become.

Portrait after portrait, I could feel tears burn the backs of my eyes.

A picture of Ian standing beside Duncan, a playful smile on his gorgeous face. The date on the back, written in an elegant script was 1786, April 22, which was shortly after Ian and Duncan's return to Braemar. His mum had caught every line of his face, the mischievous glint in his eye, and even the friendship between he and his brother.

This was the Ian I remembered.

God, I missed him.

My fingers brushed over his face and I smiled.

"He's lovely, isn't he?" Karen said softly.

"Yes," I managed, my voice hoarse.

"The handsome one is Ian, and his brother was Duncan, who is my Duncan's great, great, great, great, great grandfather."

"Hey, be kind," Duncan said, frowning.

"Everyone always talks about how lovely Ian was," Karen explained, keeping her voice lowered.

"Duncan is handsome, too," I said in Ian's brother's defense. Honestly, anyone would pale in comparison to Ian.

"Unfortunately, Ian was murdered shortly after that picture was painted. A tragedy the family never recovered from," Karen said, with a wistful smile. "It was said Duncan was heartbroken from the loss of his brother. Apparently the two were inseparable as children."

"Kade looks like Ian," I said, and everyone in the room agreed.

"That's not the bloody half of it, lass," the giant said, and I glanced at him for a second. What did he mean by that? I wondered.

I wanted to take a picture on my cell phone, to keep it close, because all I had was the drawing he had sat for, which had less detail. But I knew it would seem weird to ask. I handed the portrait over to Karen.

The rest of the portraits were of the family when they were at a celebration. There were servants, and my pulse skittered when I saw Laria in the very right-hand corner of the picture, wearing a white apron over a plain brown gown. Beside her was the man who I had seen in her visions, and the same man who had come to her the night Ian had passed over. The man at the glen who I assumed must be her dad.

"Who are all these other people?" I asked.

"Extended family, I believe...and servants, which the MacKinnons' considered family." Karen pointed to the back of the picture. "On the back she wrote each name."

I flipped over the painting. In the same perfect cursive as the other pictures, she'd written each name. The name of the man beside Laria was Randall Cummins.

Laria's last name was Sinclair. I searched the names again, and a man of average height with brown hair and eyes was her father. I didn't recall him in any of the visions or dreams. Who the hell was Randall Cummins to Laria, and why had he come to get her the night I had broken the curse and crossed Ian over?

I handed her the drawing.

Cait looked beyond bored. "Let's go to my room before you have to leave."

I helped Karen put the paintings away. I'd love to get my hands on them again, but I couldn't without it seeming strange.

After thanking Karen for showing me the paintings, I followed Cait to her room, and didn't have to look back to feel Kade watching me.

Chapter Ten

Miss Akin called an hour later, reminding me it was time to come home. Cait asked Kade if he'd drop me off and he immediately agreed, saying he needed to get his keys.

"Don't do anything I wouldn't do." Cait gave me a wink and told me she'd see me tomorrow.

I shook my head and slid my backpack on, and walked down the stairs toward the entry.

Madison met me there. Hands on hips, she said, "You see him, don't you?"

"See who?" I asked, doing my best to pretend like I had no idea what she was talking about.

"Don't bullshit me. Hanway. I know you can see and hear him."

Hanway. Wasn't that the name of the cattle thief who had been imprisoned in Braemar's dungeon centuries ago? The notorious ghost who screamed in the middle of the night. "You're right, I do see him."

She watched me closely, and I could see the mixture of excitement and trepidation in her eyes.

My heart actually picked up speed. I had found another psychic. Granted, she might only be twelve, but she could possibly help me.

"I knew it," she said under her breath, grinning from ear to ear. "That's freaking awesome."

"Who else do you see?" I asked, keeping my voice low. The last thing I needed was Kade overhearing the conversation.

"Uh, I live in a castle. I've see more ghosts than I can count." She stepped closer, lowered her voice. "But most are afraid to come around on account of the witch."

Excitement rippled through me. I wanted confirmation that we were talking about the same spirit. "Witch?"

Madison rolled her eyes. "Hanway says you know her."

Smart-ass... I couldn't help but smile. Madison reminded me of my brother.

"Do you ever speak to her?"

Madison's eyes widened and she looked at me like I was mental. "No, she's way too creepy."

"You got that right."

"You knew Ian, didn't you?"

I felt like the breath had been sucked from my lungs. "You knew Ian?"

"No, but Hanway mentioned him. You know that's the reason my mom bailed on me."

"Because of Hanway?"

"No," she said sounding exasperated. "Because I see ghosts. She thought I was losing my mind. From the time I was three I had an imaginary friend. I could tell when my mom actually started paying attention. I sometimes wonder if that's why she started doing drugs."

"You can't blame your—"

"Hey, you two," Kade said, coming down the stairs, swinging his keychain around his index finger.

"Gotta go. See ya, Williams," Madison said, rushing past us.

I was sorry to see her leave. I had so many questions to ask her. "See ya, Maddy."

The night sky was full of stars, the moon so big it looked like you could reach out and touch it. As we walked across the gravel to the Range Rover, I was excited at what I'd learned tonight, and excited that not only could I see Peter, but Hanway too.

Kade opened the passenger side door and I slid into the seat. He shut the door and then walked around the car. I glanced up, and in the shadows I swore I saw someone standing beside a tree not twenty feet from us.

At first I wondered if it was Peter, but the height wasn't right. The figure moved slightly, enough for me to make out long hair and a gown. Laria's face looked even paler than I remembered, and yet she was as solid as any human.

I immediately locked the door.

Kade got in, buckled up, and turned the key in the ignition. I looked back at the trees and Laria was gone. Chill bumps appeared on my arms and I felt a familiar sense of dread come over me. Swallowing past the lump in my throat, I glanced in the side mirror and swore I could make out someone sitting in the backseat, directly behind me.

Someone with long brown hair.

I wanted to reach for Kade's hand, but I didn't dare. I was frozen with fear.

"So...you made it through a night with my family."

"It was nice meeting them," I said, my heartbeat a roar in my ears.

"I'm sorry about your mum. That must have been difficult to go through."

"Thanks, it was difficult, but I'm better now."

Couldn't he feel the freezing cold?

Apparently not, because he stared at me and smiled. "I'm really glad you're here, Riley."

Memories of a similar conversation I'd had with Ian came back to me. "Thanks, I am, too."

We started down the long driveway, and this was one time I was glad it wouldn't take long to get to my house.

Icy hands clenched my shoulders tightly, slowly pulling me back against the seat. Firm, long fingers dug into my skin at the collarbone.

I tried to lean forward, to get away from the hands that held me firmly against the seat. I couldn't budge. A second later those same hands were around my neck, squeezing tight.

I started choking.

Kade's eyes widened, and he swerved onto the shoulder of the road and slammed the car into Park. "Riley, are you all right?"

I felt dizzy, like I was going to black out at any second.

I heard a voice, but I couldn't make out what they said. Like faint whispering running in a loop over another voice.

"Riley." Kade's hand was on my shoulder, and I could hear the alarm in his tone.

The next second I was released, just like that.

I took a deep breath and looked behind me.

The backseat was empty.

Kade followed my gaze, and his brows furrowed.

"Sorry," I said, rubbing my neck. "I don't know what just happened."

Not the best explanation, but it would have to suffice. I wasn't about to tell him I was being stalked by a malevolent spirit. For some reason I didn't think that would go over so well.

After the fifth time asking me if I was all right, and me assuring him I was, he drove me home, and once there he walked me to the front door.

"I'm glad you came over. I hope you will again."

"I'd like that." I reached for the door handle. "Thanks for the ride."

"You're welcome. I'll see you tomorrow."

"See you tomorrow," I said, glancing at the car and wondering if Laria was hiding in the backseat. "Hey, text me when you get home, okay?"

The sides of his mouth lifted in a boyish grin. "Okay."

"Good night." I waited until he was in the car and pulling out of the driveway before I walked into the inn, shut the door, and locked it behind me. Aside from Laria's chokehold on my neck, tonight had been a good night, and now that I knew Hanway was in residence at the castle, I had questions for him and Madison. She knew Laria, and was well aware that she was a malevolent spirit. Although I hesitated to get a twelve-year-old involved in my problems, I had little choice. I needed help, and now that Anne Marie had skipped town, I needed someone to bounce thoughts off of.

I climbed the steps to my room, trying to gather my thoughts.

I opened the door to my room and my breath left me in a rush.

On the wall in red ink was the word CUTTER written in six-inch letters. In the middle of my bed sat the matchbox I'd made sure had been tossed in the trash.

Chapter Eleven

It was the first football game of the season, and I had a tough time keeping my focus on the game. Last night Laria had shaken me up by trying to choke me. Coming home to find the writing on the wall and the razor blades back on my bed had been too much.

I'd spent thirty minutes before I fell asleep scrubbing the walls. The red paint had come off easily enough, but had left a pink tint to the wall. And the razor blades—that had been a different battle altogether.

Focusing on my mom, I asked for her help. As expected whenever I connected with her, a sense of calm fell over me. I had honestly thought my desire to cut would fade with time, but having the razor blades show up again and again reminded me I had far from won that battle. The desire to cut ate at me, and for a minute last night I had almost put the blades into the back of my sock drawer, where I'd kept them before I promised never to cut again.

Even last night I'd had a dream about cutting, so first thing this morning I had put the matchbox and blades into a plastic grocery bag, tied it tight and put it in the outdoor trash can.

"Your boyfriend is looking hot," Megan said, pulling me back to the present.

She was right. Kade was looking hot. Dressed in his navy and white uniform, he put every other guy to shame.

Megan kept glancing at Shane. I knew she was crushing on him, but I didn't say anything. She loved Milo. I knew that, and an innocent crush wouldn't hurt anything. Or so I hoped.

The bleachers were packed, and I saw Mr. and Mrs. MacKinnon sitting front and center. Both waved at me, and I waved back. Madison sat beside them, earbuds in, and she had her head down, apparently texting. She glanced up when Karen had waved at me, did a little head nod in acknowledgment, and looked back at her phone.

I desperately wanted to talk to her, to finish our discussion about Ian. She knew about him, and although she said she hadn't seen Ian, it was obvious Hanway had talked about him.

Cait, who had been talking to a group of Emo kids, including Joni, joined us, sliding in beside Cassandra. Cassandra had smuggled in a baby bottle of liquor and had poured it into her soda bottle in the car. I didn't think getting started right away was a good thing, but I wasn't going to be a buzzkill either.

She offered me a drink but I shook my head. I wasn't about to get drunk, or even buzzed for that matter, especially when I had a crazy spirit out to kill me.

I was actually relieved when Megan declined the drink as well, saying she didn't feel like being hung over for our drive into Aberdeen tomorrow to shop for dresses for Milo's party.

Cait went for it though, which surprised me with her parents nearby.

The horn blasted and the game started.

Shane wasn't on the field. I hoped the coach played him, despite the fight he'd been in the other day. Every once in a while he would glance up into the stands, and I could see him looking at Joni. He didn't say much about her, but I knew he liked her, and I could tell she was into him too.

Loud laughter brought my attention to Dana and her crew who were sitting two rows down from us. She kept glancing back over her shoulder at me.

Megan squeezed my arm. "Just ignore her."

I nodded, and focused on the game and on Kade. He handled the ball with incredible skill, and he was fast on his feet. Within the first minute he had an assist.

Football in the U.K. was at a whole different level than it was back home. Shane was good, but he had his work cut out for him here. If anything, these guys would make him a better player.

I glanced at Cait. "Your brother is incredible."

"He lives and breathes football," she said. "He's been in junior league since he was six."

As the minutes ticked by, it became more and more obvious that Kade was the star of the team. His coach constantly talked to him. Kade had his hands on his hips and nodded, looking completely focused. When the coach finally sat him out, he grabbed a towel, wiped his face, and glanced up into the stands. I actually held my breath as he scanned the crowd, and when his gaze landed on me, he nodded and smiled softly.

Dana waved at him, and I felt myself blush. I had sworn he was looking at me.

Megan laughed under her breath. "For the record, he was waving at you, not Dana."

I was glad Megan thought he was looking at me, too. That way I wasn't just seeing what I wanted to see. Last night he had texted me back when he'd gotten home, telling me again how great the night had been and how his family really liked me. He'd also mentioned getting together soon. I'd told him I'd like that.

Megan's eyes widened. "Oh shit, Ri. Your nose is bleeding."

I lifted my hand to my nose, and was stunned when my hand came back with blood.

She fished in her purse, pulled out a small package of tissue, and handed me one.

I wiped away the blood.

"You snorting pills?" Cassandra asked, lifting a brow.

It took me a second to realize she was serious. "No."

My nose kept bleeding, and I had no choice but to excuse myself and go to the bathroom. Just my luck two of Dana's buddies stood at the sinks, putting makeup on. Seeing me, they went quiet.

One of the girls, a tall brunette touched her nose. "Uh, you have blood on your nose, *sweetheart*."

I bit the inside of my lip.

I went into the stall and blew my nose. I couldn't believe the amount of blood that was on the tissue. I unrolled more toilet paper and dropped the blood-soaked tissue in the toilet.

A minute or so later the bathroom door opened and closed, and I sighed in relief, glad to be alone.

I went to the sink, lifted my chin and pinched my nose at the bridge.

The light overhead started to flicker. The plastic cover over the bulbs was yellowed from time, and a bulb flashed a few times before it went out altogether.

Nice.

At least there looked to be one more bulb. It didn't give off a lot of light, but enough for me to see that my nosebleed had stopped.

I turned on the water, cupped my hands beneath the stream and cleaned off the little bit of blood that had caked around my nostrils.

The light overhead popped and I stood in total darkness.

An overwhelming sense of fear gripped me and I immediately made a move for the door, but I was grabbed from behind. A scream died on my lips. A second later my head slammed into the sink. Cold water had been turned on full blast, and firm hands held my head down.

I tried to fight back, to get my head up out of the water that was starting to pool in the basin, but the attacker was stronger than me.

My face was freezing and I couldn't breathe. On the verge of passing out, I panicked and used all my strength to fight back. I pushed back with all my might.

Suddenly, the light went on.

"What the hell are you doing?" I heard someone ask, their voice sounding like it was coming from a long way away.

I had my hands on either side of the sink basin, my bangs completely wet, and I had makeup running down my face.

"Riley?"

It was Dana. For the first time in my life I was happy to see her. Happy that someone had walked in before I'd been killed. And I had no doubt Laria, or whoever it had been, had tried to kill me.

The situation looked insane. My hair was wet. The basin was clear...and there wasn't even a stopper in the drain. How was that possible?

"You had a nosebleed, I hear," she said, taking a tentative step closer.

"Allergies." Even my voice was shaky. "I couldn't get it to stop."

Her expression alone said she thought I was psychotic, but I didn't care. At least the nosebleed was one way to explain why my hair and face were wet.

I felt chills rush up my back at the same time someone growled in my ear and I jumped. I glanced over my shoulder. No one was there—just Dana standing by the door, watching me like I'd lost my mind.

"Um, it looks like you took a bath," she said, lips quirked.

I know I looked like hell. Her expression just confirmed it. Hitting the dryer button, I lowered my head and made an attempt to at least get my bangs dry and keep from shaking. Laria, or whoever had just tried to drown me, wasn't messing around this time. I had to have help. I needed answers. I needed someone who understood what I was going through.

When I finished drying my bangs, I wiped the makeup from under my eyes with a tissue.

Dana finally stepped closer, in front of the mirror and applied lip gloss, all the while watching me. I wanted to ask her if she had any mascara I could borrow, but I couldn't bring myself to ask her. It's not like I wore a lot of makeup anyway. Plus, with the way my hands were trembling, I'd probably just make more of a mess.

"So...you like Kade?"

There it was—the million dollar question.

"He's nice," I said, doing my best to fix my hair. At least I didn't look like a drowned rat any longer.

She dropped her gloss into her purse. "Yep, he's really nice. A word to the wise though—he doesn't get attached for long."

And yet that fact didn't seem to stop her from going for him.

"See you later," I said, walking toward the door.

"Hey, if you ever want to hang out sometime, give me a call."

Was she serious?

"You want my mobile number?" she asked, pulling her cell out of her pocket. I wasn't about to give her my phone number.

I was saved from having to respond when Cait walked in. "I was wondering if you fell in."

I was so relieved to see her, I almost hugged her. "I was just heading back."

"Are you okay?" she asked, tilting her head to the side, confirming I looked as horrible as I felt.

"I'm fine," I said, a complete lie since I was shaken up.

"Hey Cait," Dana said, perking up immediately.

"Dana," Cait replied, with a stiff nod. She slid her hand around my elbow and pulled me out of the bathroom. As we walked toward the bleachers, she watched me closely. "You're like Maddy, aren't you, Riley?"

My stomach tightened. "What do you mean?"

"You can see the dead."

Had Madison said something to her? I wondered.

"I've lived with Maddy long enough to know that she's not talking to an imaginary friend. There's someone actually there. I saw the same look in your eyes last night while we were eating, and after, when you were looking at pictures. Who was there with us?"

I was reluctant to say too much. After all, she lived in the castle and I didn't want to be the reason she couldn't sleep at night.

"That's why you wouldn't sit in the chair, was it? Because someone else was already sitting there."

Very good.

I was so used to being quiet about my abilities, and honestly, I was terrified of Cait saying something to Kade. Then again, I wasn't going to lie to my friend, especially when she knew the truth.

"The ghost Maddy talks to is Hanway," I said before I could stop myself.

"Hanway," she said, her eyes going wide. "Wait, that's the ghost who tore his nails off trying to get out of the dungeon, right?" She sounded almost excited.

I nodded. "Yes, but for the record, his nails looked fine to me."

"Who else have you seen?"

I wasn't ready to tell her about Laria. Plus, I wasn't going to tell her I'd been in the castle before the other night. I wasn't so sure she'd be okay with that. If the tables were turned, I'm not so sure I would be okay with it either. "There's a boy named Peter at our school."

I saw some of the fear leave her face. "A boy...like how old?"

"Peter's eleven."

"So bloody young," she said absently. "What's it like—to be able to talk to someone who's dead?"

No one had asked me that question before. "I guess it's kind of like talking to you right now."

Her brows formed a straight line. "Oh, come on."

"I'm serious. The dead are just like us...they're just invisible to the majority."

"I wish I could see them."

"No you don't," I said matter-of-factly.

She went quiet when Dana walked past us, chin lifted high.

We returned to the stands, but I couldn't focus at all on the game. I was too shaky, and I kept expecting Laria to appear, to reach around my neck again and choke me. I clapped every time our team scored, and was disappointed Shane didn't get a chance to play.

"You ready?" Megan asked, when there was five minutes left on the clock.

I nodded, ready to leave, yet dreading what waited for me this time when I got home.

Chapter Twelve

Aberdeen was packed on Saturday afternoon. Having grown up in Portland, I missed the sights and sounds of the city. The *pulse,* as my mom would call it. She was right—I felt more alive, and it felt nice to get away from Braemar, and away from Laria, who was becoming more aggressive and pissing me off more by the day.

I was glad Megan and Cassandra had asked me to come along. I needed the break, and plus, it would be nice to wear a new dress to Milo's party.

I'd come to appreciate Cassandra, even though she sometimes could use an edit button. But there was a part of me that liked her blatant honesty, especially since I could never be that way.

The crosswalk light turned, illuminating the pedestrian sign, and we crossed the street. A car at the crosswalk honked at the driver in front of him.

Tempers ran high, especially in the city where everyone was in a hurry to get where they were going. It didn't matter if you were halfway around the world. People were people.

"Here we are," Cassandra said, stopping at the double doors of a store called *Lady Haute.* The woman at the counter gave me the once over, and I swear to God she actually sniffed. When her gaze shifted to Cassandra she completely changed. Smiling from ear to ear, she rushed over. "How are you, my dear?"

"So fake," Megan said under her breath.

If the woman heard her, she didn't seem to care. She was too busy fawning all over Cassandra. Even though I had grown up in an upper middle class family, my mom rarely shopped at high end stores.

To be honest though, the extra attention was kind of nice.

I browsed the racks and found a handful of dresses to try on.

The dressing room had an unforgiving three-way mirror, which made critiquing each dress easy. The majority were too tight and I knew I'd feel self-conscious wearing any of them.

Cassandra didn't pull any punches when it came to giving her opinion either, especially with Megan who had a tough time finding the right dress because of her big boobs.

I found a flouncy white sundress with spaghetti straps on the clearance rack. There was an innocence about it I liked, and the gathering over the bust didn't hurt either.

"What are you—twelve?" Cassandra asked, looking downright disgusted with my choice.

I stared back at my reflection in the mirror. "Is it that bad?"

"I think it's adorable," Megan said, frowning at Cassandra. "Not all of us want to look like sluts."

"Hey, be nice now," Cassandra said, tugging at the hem of a body-hugging black lace dress with a nude underlining that made her look like she was naked beneath. "I'm out to snag a man, and you can't do that with a dress a tween would wear."

Maybe she was right—maybe I would get more attention if I

dressed sexy, but I would be uncomfortable and it would show.

No, I needed to stay true to who I was. With my mind made up, I took the dress up to the cashier.

Cassandra glanced at the shopkeeper. "Put it on my bill."

"Cassandra, that's no—"

"I'm paying," she said, cutting me off. Her expression alone said to not argue.

I sat in one of the chairs in the dressing room while Cassandra and Megan continued to try on dresses. I wished Cait would have come with us. I would have liked to have talked to her more about ghosts and Madison's abilities. I hoped she didn't mention the psychic stuff to Kade. It was hard enough for me to understand, let alone having to explain to someone else.

I wondered if he did find out, if that would change how he felt about me. I didn't even want to think about having to bring up the cutting. Even if it was in my recent past, it was still my past, and I hated the thought of him judging me.

By the time we finished shopping for shoes and accessories, it was nearly three o'clock, and we were all excited about Milo's party. Megan seemed a little nervous. I wondered if she was worried what people were saying about Milo's band. I could only hope that Milo proved everyone wrong.

We drove in silence, listening to music, and every once in a while we talked about someone at school. I couldn't help myself. "So... what can you tell me about Dana?"

"Total bitch." Cassandra pulled the visor down and put on lipstick. "She started dating when she was like thirteen. She's been around, that one."

And she wanted Kade.

"Oh, and she's a total bottle redhead and lies about it." Cassandra made it sound like coloring your hair was a crime.

Megan glanced at me. "See, I told you."

"Honestly, I wouldn't worry about Dana when it comes to Kade." Cassandra ran a finger over her teeth, scrubbing off lipstick. "I would worry about her spreading shit about you though. She's made life miserable for more than one person, myself included. When she wants something, she goes for it...and she's bloody ruthless."

I thought of the razor blade in my locker, the looks she gave me at the glen with the scratches, and then last night with the nosebleed.

It started misting and Megan turned on the wiper blades, leaving a blurry white film on the windshield. "Shit, I just made it worse." It took a good dozen swipes for the windshield to finally clear.

"People will believe what they choose to believe," I said, and Cassandra nodded in agreement.

A song came on the radio and Cassandra started singing. Megan joined in and soon I was singing along. I liked how comfortable I had become with them, and I dreaded the day they found out about my cutting.

Megan stopped singing and leaned closer to the steering wheel. "What the hell is that?"

On the right side of the road there was a woman, sitting in a meadow with her back to us, arms wrapped around her legs, rocking back and forth.

My heart slammed against my breastbone. Even from a distance I knew who it was. Long brown hair fell to the ground, and I recognized Laria's green gown.

"Fucking creepy," Cassandra said under her breath.

Megan slowed the car to a crawl. "What do you think she's doing?"

"Don't stop, Megan," I said, slamming the door lock down. "Please."

I could tell by Megan's expression that I had surprised her by my reaction. She frowned at me. "Look at her. She obviously needs help. She's sitting in the middle of a bloody field, for God's sake."

"What if it's a setup? I mean for all we know she could have buddies waiting in the wings ready to carjack us and do who knows what else to us."

Megan glanced at Cassandra.

Cassandra's eyes were enormous. "I'm with Ri on this one. No fucking way are we stopping."

"Maybe we should at least ask her if she needs anything." Megan pulled the car to the side of the road.

"We'll call 999 when we get mobile service," Cassandra suggested.

My dad had already told me that dialing three nines was the equivalent to 911 in the U.S. "Just drive, Megan," I said under my breath. "Please just drive."

Megan pulled back onto the road, her jaw clenched tight. Cassandra and I shared a look and she shrugged. We drove in silence for the next five miles. I tried to take heart in the fact that both of them had seen Laria too, and yet I couldn't shake the feeling that Laria wasn't finished with us.

Cassandra poked Megan in the arm a few times and she finally caved and smiled, shaking her head. "I just hope we don't see anything on the news later about a girl who is missing. I'll never forgive myself."

"Don't worry, you won't," I said, wishing I could tell them the girl was a ghost, and that she was stalking me and making my life a nightmare. Maybe then she wouldn't feel so bad.

I recognized a house we passed and knew we were within miles of Braemar. What a relief. I just wanted to get home, take a hot shower and get ready for the party.

"No fuckin' way."

I followed Megan's gaze and my heart fell to my toes.

Laria was standing on the roadside, head down, hair covering most of her face, hands at her side.

"What...the...hell." All the color drained from Cassandra's face. "How did she get all the way here? I mean, no one else could have picked her up and dropped her off. We never stopped and no cars have passed us."

I wanted to tell them everything I knew about Laria, and yet the words died on my lips. They would think I was crazy, and I felt like I was cracking a bit now that she'd returned. They probably were already suspecting that I took drugs after last night's drama in the school bathroom.

"Don't you dare stop, Megan," I said, not wanting to look, and yet not being able to turn away.

Megan's fingers tightened around the steering wheel. "I have to."

"I swear to God, I'll leave you here if you get out of this car," Cassandra said, her voice rising with every word.

"Please don't, Megan," I said, feeling desperate. "You don't know what she's capable of."

Megan frowned at me. "What are you talking about?"

Both Cassandra and Megan were watching me like I was crazy.

"I mean, I don't trust it. This is wrong. Cassandra's right. Think about it—how could she have traveled so far in such a short period of time? It's impossible."

I could see Megan processing what I was saying, but she shook her head. "Sorry, I have to stop. I can't live with myself if I don't."

She pulled over and stopped the car. I slid my hands down my face, unsure of what to do. This was bad. Megan stepped out of the car. Immediately, Cassandra slid into the driver's side, and shut and locked the door.

Fear knotted my insides.

"Are you all right?" Megan called.

Damn it. I couldn't leave Megan to deal with Laria alone, especially when it wasn't Megan that Laria wanted.

I slid into the front passenger seat and unlocked the door.

"What are you doing?" Cassandra asked, alarm in her voice.

"I can't let her go alone."

"Quick, look in the glove box and see if there's any pepper spray."

I would have laughed if I wasn't so scared. Pepper spray wasn't about to stop Laria. I looked anyway. No pepper spray.

When Megan started walking toward her, I held my breath and opened the car door.

"Don't get out of the car," Cassandra said, and there was no mistaking the panic in her voice.

Megan walked toward Laria. My heartbeat was a roar in my ears as I stepped from the car. "Megan, please come back."

Only a few feet separated Megan from Laria and I started running to catch up with her.

But I was too late. Megan reached out to touch Laria on the shoulder. I could see Laria lift her head slowly.

Megan didn't move. She just stood there, her shoulders lifting with every inhale.

"Megan?" I said.

Laria reached for Megan, and then disappeared in the blink of an eye.

Slowly, Megan turned and walked toward me, stopping beside me. "Did you just see what I saw?"

"Yes, she disappeared."

Megan nodded and swallowed hard. "Get in the car," she said, her voice intense.

She didn't have to tell me twice.

Cassandra scrambled into the backseat and for once was silent.

I got back in the car. Megan locked her door, and then reached across me to lock my door. She started the engine. "I should have listened to you both. I shouldn't have stopped."

"Ya think?" Cassandra said, looking out the back window. "I mean, where the hell did she go?"

Megan took a deep breath, and then putting on her blinker, pulled onto the road.

Chapter Thirteen

The party at Milo's house was in full swing when I arrived with Megan, who had said very little to me since picking me up. I wanted to mention Laria and what we'd seen earlier on the way home, hoping maybe she'd ask me about ghosts in general. Apparently she was still pissed off or lost in her own thoughts, because she remained silent the rest of the way to Milo's house.

Cait met us at the door and she was quick to inform me that Dana and her friends had dropped in uninvited and dressed to kill. That's not at all what I wanted to hear. Even worse, Dana wore one of those bandage dresses that hugged every curve and left nothing to the imagination. I immediately removed my sweater, and smoothed the skirt of my sundress.

Maybe Cassandra had been right. Maybe I could have kicked up the sex appeal a bit more.

At least I was having a good hair night. I couldn't say the same for Dana, who had gone with an updo that made her nose look bigger.

Avoiding Dana and her friends, I slipped out onto the back patio where Megan sat with Milo, Richie and Shane. I hadn't talked to Shane, and seeing me, he smiled, which was a relief. I never knew which Shane I was going to get.

Shane checked out Cait and I could tell she knew it, too—talking to me, but watching my brother from the corner of her eye. I totally got it. I knew she was fascinated by him. I couldn't very well say anything since I was into her brother.

Speaking of—Kade walked outside. "There you are," he said, his gaze shifting slowly over me. "Wow, you look beautiful. I like the dress."

I smiled, happy by the compliments.

He wore a light blue dress shirt rolled up at the elbows, acid-washed jeans, the familiar Celtic cross necklace, and a braided leather bracelet around his wrist. I loved his large hands, the long fingers.

Cait lingered for all of two seconds before walking over to Shane.

"I looked for you after the game last night," Kade said. "I wish you would have stayed. I wanted to give you a ride home."

Despite the fact I would have loved the time alone with him, I was glad I'd left early, especially since I'd been shaken up by Laria and looked like hell.

"Maybe next time," I said.

His eyes brightened. "Definitely."

As much as I'd like to believe he hadn't heard about my little episode in the bathroom, I knew he had. It was just a matter of time, especially with Dana slinking around. "Congratulations on winning the game, by the way. I'm not sure if anyone has ever told you this—but you're pretty good at football."

"Thanks," he said, a smile tugging at his lips. Man, I loved those dimples.

Milo and Richie walked past us. Richie pinched my butt, which surprised me. Richie always seemed to be the laid-back one. Tonight his hair wasn't in its usual ponytail, but down around his shoulders. The red waves were shiny; the kind of hair most girls would kill to have. "You look hot, Ri."

"Thanks, Richie."

The nerve in Kade's jaw twitched as he watched Richie's retreating back.

"A friend of Shane's," I said needlessly.

"He should learn to keep his hands to himself."

Oh my God, he was actually jealous. "He's harmless, really."

Taking a deep breath, Kade blurted, "When can we hang out?"

Exhilaration worked its way up my spine. "Tomorrow works for me."

A slow smile spread across his face. "Name the time and I'll be there."

I was so elated. Finally we'd have time alone together without buddies or family hanging around.

A loud screech from the bass speakers came from inside the house, and Megan walked up beside me. "Come on. They're ready to play."

Everyone filed into the house.

The room was packed around Milo and two other guys, whose instruments were set up in the corner of the room, ready to play. I knew Milo had been in a band for years, Megan had said, and I was excited to hear him play, and a little nervous too. I wanted him to be good, especially since people at school had been talking shit about his singing abilities.

Johan came forward and handed Kade a beer. He nodded at me. "Riley."

I nodded. "Hey, Johan."

"You look nice," he said, tipping his head back as he took a drink.

Kade shifted on his feet.

I'm sure Kade knew I'd spent some time with Johan over the summer. I remembered Ian's jealousy, and I could see that same jealousy mirrored in Kade's eyes now.

"Come on, Riley." Megan sounded kind of irritated with me, which surprised me since she'd been encouraging when it came to Kade.

She was already disappearing into the crowd, making her way toward the front, where there definitely wasn't room for two broad-shouldered guys.

Kade must have seen my hesitation, because he said, "Go ahead. I'll meet up with you later."

"Sounds good."

I followed Megan into the crowd and to the front of the makeshift stage. Milo stepped up, grabbed the microphone, and said, "Testing, testing, one, two, three."

Everyone clapped.

Milo smiled at Megan and she grinned. Tonight she'd worn bright red lipstick and dark makeup, which went great with her black dress.

"We can only sing a few songs tonight—else my neighbors will lose their shite. Here goes," Milo said, sliding a guitar strap around his neck and playing the opening chords of a catchy riff that had everyone jumping up and down to the beat.

Cassandra and Cait wedged in between us.

Milo started singing and I was shocked. He was *really* good. Megan didn't take her eyes off of him as he played the guitar, his fingers moving seamlessly over the strings. I had to admit there was something incredibly sexy about a guy playing a guitar, and Milo fit lead singer to a T.

Plus, he had an awesome camaraderie going with the audience, and he was fun to watch. "That's his older brother on drums," Cassandra said, nodding to a thin guy with long brown hair, tattoos and gauged ears. "His cousin's on bass." The cousin had a similar look to Milo with spiky black hair, and he wore guy-liner well, making his piercing light eyes even more intense.

"I can see the family resemblance," I said.

During one of the songs, a head-banging anthem about a girl who had done a boy wrong appropriately called *Soul Killer*, I looked over my shoulder to find Kade. He stood by the door, nodding in time to the music. At his side was Dana, who went up on her tiptoes to say something in his ear. She leaned in, her boobs rubbing against his arm.

My nails dug into my palms.

Without looking at her, he shook his head, and continued to watch the band. His gaze abruptly shifted to me. I smiled and turned back toward the stage, and told myself to not worry about what Dana was doing or saying.

At the end of the three-song set, the crowd clapped and yelled their approval. Milo and his band mates beamed. As Milo set his guitar down, Megan threw her arms around his neck and hugged him tight. "You were so good, love."

"Really?" Milo glanced from Megan to me, Cait and Cassandra.

Cassandra nodded. "You were bloody brilliant."

"Incredible," Cait said.

He looked at me, brows lifted high.

"You were great, Milo," I said. "I'm so impressed."

"Thanks, Ri. That means a lot."

He turned to Megan, who planted a kiss on him, which he eagerly accepted.

Shane clapped him on the back, and Milo hugged him.

"Come with me," Cassandra said, pulling me and Cait by the arms toward the bathroom. She shut the door behind us and locked it.

"What's up?" Cait asked, setting her drink on the counter.

"Johan asked if he could call me sometime," Cassandra blurted, looking from me to Cait and back again.

That surprised me. Johan had made it clear that he and Cassandra weren't together, but even more, it seemed like Tom really liked her.

"What did you say?" I asked, hoping Cait would give her two cents, but she remained silent.

Cassandra pulled mascara out of her purse and freshened up her makeup. "I said sure."

Cait's mouth opened in disgust. "Oh my God, seriously?"

I had a feeling all Johan wanted was a booty call, but I wasn't going to tell her that. After all, maybe I was wrong. What did I know about guys anyway? The most important thing was to be a good friend, and at least be encouraging. "Hey, all you can do is see what happens, right?"

"Right." She leaned her hip against the counter and looked at Cait, her eyes narrowed. "Come on, say what's on your mind."

"I think he's buzzed and wants a piece of ass."

"Nice," Cassandra said, and I could tell the words stung.

Cait shrugged. "Sorry, Cass, I'm not going to sugarcoat it. I just don't want to see you get hurt, that's all. Like Riley says though...see what happens. But just be smart."

I could tell Cassandra's excitement had waned. She glanced at me. "I told Cait about the ghost we saw on the ride home from Aberdeen. It was so fucking creepy," Cassandra said, glancing at her reflection and running her fingers through her blonde curls.

I nodded in agreement. "It was creepy."

"I wished I'd been there." Cait took a sip of her drink. "I always miss out, damn it."

"Maybe next time your mum will actually let you go with us. She needs to get over the fact you have older friends who want to hang out with you."

It made sense that Karen would be overprotective, especially since we were all a year older than Cait. She reminded me of my mom when I'd started hanging out with Ashley, a party girl who was older than me.

A knock at the door made us all jump and we laughed.

"Just a second," Cassandra said, pinching her cheeks.

She glanced at us, ran her hands down the lace of her dress and flung back her hair. "Watch out, Johan."

As the night wore on, the crowd dwindled down to a group of about twenty of us. Unfortunately, Dana and her clique were part of that group. They wouldn't leave for anything, and the problem was...my curfew of midnight was looming.

Milo took a fork and tapped it against his glass. "Hey everyone. Let's play a game."

Seriously? What was it with the Scottish and their games?

"Never have I ever!" a few people said at the same time.

Never have I ever? Even the name made me nervous. Then again, it couldn't be much worse than Truth or Dare.

"What's Never Have I Ever?" I asked Kade, who took a seat beside me.

"The first player says something he has never done—like, Never have I ever ate a bug. Then everyone who has eaten a bug would take a drink."

"So basically if you've done it, you drink?"

He nodded. "Exactly."

Milo went around the room with a pitcher and filled up everyone's glass with beer. Joni had arrived after Milo's band played, and now she sat by Shane. "Since it's my party, I'll go first. Never have I ever—gone skinny-dipping."

Dana and her buddies were the only girls who took a drink, which brought whistles and laughter. Dana actually looked at Kade and smiled shyly.

Ugh, I had to look away.

Next it was Richie's turn. "Never have I ever been caught shoplifting."

The whole group laughed, and a few people drank, including Cassandra and Megan.

Next it was Shane's turn. "Never have I ever—lied about my weight."

All the girls took a drink and Milo gave Shane a wink. I was beginning to get the idea that the boys did everything they could to get the girls drunk.

"Never have I ever—kissed someone and regretted it," Joni said giving Shane a coy grin.

Nearly every girl took a drink, and a few guys as well.

One of Dana's friends went next. "Never have I ever—slept with someone."

Everyone drank...except for me. The only other virgin in the room smiled at me and nodded.

I could feel my cheeks turn warm as everyone zeroed in on me. Apparently they didn't know many nearly seventeen-year-old virgins. Even Shane looked surprised.

"Nice!" Milo said, biting his lip ring and wiggling his brows. He glanced at Kade and winked.

I didn't see Kade's reaction.

"Never have I ever—snorted drugs," the girl next to Dana said, looking straight at me. She slid a French manicured finger around the rim of her glass.

Half the group drank, which surprised me a little. One thing about the game was you could find out a lot about a person.

I was starting to sweat it...because I knew damn well what Dana would say next. She would ask about cutting. I wouldn't put it past her, especially since she'd made the comment about my welts at the glen, and then there had been the razor blade in my locker the next day. Granted, she couldn't have put it back in my textbook after I'd tossed it, but still...she knew.

I glanced at Shane, who was watching me closely. He must have seen my apprehension because he abruptly stood up. "Sorry to bail on you guys, but Riley and I have to head out. We have fifteen minutes to get home."

It would take five to get home, but I wasn't about to argue.

"But we're not finished," Dana said, clearly pissed that she wouldn't get her chance to call me out, which only confirmed my suspicions.

"You need to have a serious conversation with your dad about your curfew, dude. This is ridiculous," Milo said, pulling a cigarette out of his pocket and heading for the door. "I'll see you tomorrow, Williams." He looked at me and winked. "You too, Virgin Mary."

I suppose there were worse names to be called than Virgin Mary.

"See ya, Milo."

I said goodbye to Megan, who didn't budge from her spot. Cassandra walked up and gave me a hug, Cait right on her heels.

Kade followed me to the door, and helped me with my sweater. "Let me drive you home, Riley."

I had hair tucked inside my sweater, and he reached up and pulled it loose. It was a sweet gesture, and he surprised me when his fingers lingered, brushing a strand between finger and thumb.

"You sure?"

He nodded.

"I'll catch a ride with Joni's sister," Shane said, flashing a smile.

I told my friends goodnight and followed Kade to his car. The whole way home I felt him watching me. "So, tomorrow...should I bring a movie?"

After a long day of walking around Aberdeen, I was ready for a movie day, especially with Kade. "Sure, that would be great."

"Any suggestions?"

I shook my head. "Um, not really. Just no action movies."

He laughed and a little shiver raced up my spine. I loved his laugh.

I pushed the door open, stepped out, and pulled my sweater tighter around me.

I was nearly to the door when Kade shouted, "Just a sec, you forgot something."

What did I forget? I had my purse and sweater?

He was in front of me a second later, hands empty. Leaning in, he kissed me softly.

A warm glow spread through my body. He had one hand at the nape of my neck, and the other he rested on my hip, pulling me closer to him.

I slid my arms around his waist, my hands splaying against his back, feeling the play of muscles there. He deepened the kiss. He tasted sweet, like mint.

Someone honked as they drove by, but neither of us broke the kiss.

I gave a small groan, and he smiled against my lips.

He pulled away slowly. His hand cupped my face, his thumb brushing along my jaw line. "I've wanted to do that since the first time we met."

"I've wanted you to do that, too."

The entryway light flicked on and I stepped away from him. "I gotta go."

"See you tomorrow," he said, giving me one final peck before I walked inside the inn.

Chapter Fourteen

I didn't wake until after ten the next morning and immediately grabbed my phone. There were two missed messages—both from Cassandra, both mentioning Kade.

I found it odd that Megan hadn't called. She had been acting a little off last night, and I wanted to make sure that we were okay.

I didn't get why she was still so pissed about the Laria thing. I had told her not to stop the car but so had Cassandra. Oh well, it's not like she'd been particularly friendly to anyone last night, except for Milo.

I called Cassandra back, and listened to her tell me about the rest of the night. I was surprised when she said Kade hadn't returned to the party after dropping me off. That made me happy. She mentioned that Dana kept watching the door, and finally took off with her friends at one.

"Have you heard from Megan?" I asked.

"She won't pick up my calls," she said, and I breathed a sigh of relief. "Still pissed off about the ghost sighting, I guess."

I couldn't understand why she would be pissed at us about that, aside from the fact we'd let her face the ghost alone.

"Do you believe in ghosts?" I asked, knowing I needed to tread lightly.

"Of course. My grandpa haunts my grandma's house to this day...and he's been dead since before I was born."

Maybe one day I could come clean to my friends about my abilities, but not today. I heard footsteps coming from Shane's room. I glanced at the clock. Kade would be here soon. "I need to get a shower. Can I call you later?"

"Sure, what are you doing today?"

"Kade's coming over."

She let out a loud gasp, and then laughed under her breath. "Damn, he's not wasting any time, is he?"

"I'll call you later."

"Sounds good."

Thirty minutes later, I was ready to blow-dry my hair when the doorbell rang.

Miss Akin didn't answer it, and I didn't hear Shane, so I quickly towel-dried my hair and ran my fingers through the straggly mess before I rushed down the steps.

I whipped open the door.

It was Kade. Wearing a white V-neck T-shirt, low-riding jeans and white sneakers.

I swallowed hard, aware of what I must look like. Thank God at least I'd thrown on jeans and a navy tank top.

"I know I'm early.

"That's okay." I stepped back, covered the scars on my elbow with my hand. "You want to come in?"

"Is it okay?"

He closed the door behind him. He reached up, his hand easing into my hair, his thumb brushing over my lower lip. "I can't stop thinking about you."

I couldn't help but smile. I was so glad he felt the same way about me as I did about him. My arms slid around his broad shoulders. "I can't stop thinking about you, either."

His gaze shifted to my lips, and I don't know which one of us leaned in first, but we kissed, our mouths fusing together, his tongue brushing along the seam of my mouth.

I opened to him, and he moaned low in his throat, a sound that sent a spike of pleasure through me. My back was up against the wall a second later, and I was left completely breathless as he lifted me up. My legs wrapped around his waist, and he held me there with one hand on my bottom, the other curling around the back of my neck.

I could hear his heart pounding as loud as mine.

A door opened somewhere in the house and I groaned inwardly. Kade slowly eased me to the ground. "Is your dad here?" he whispered, putting some distance between us.

"Riley, can you help me with the groceries please?" Miss Akin yelled from the kitchen.

I sighed in relief. "I'll be right there, Miss A."

Kade smiled, and that smile heated the blood in my veins.

"Come on," I said with a smile, walking for the kitchen when he caught my hand.

I glanced back over my shoulder. "What?" The word hadn't left my mouth when he kissed me hard. When he pulled back I instantly recognized that dark, heavy-lidded look in his eyes. That expression left me breathless. He wanted me as much as I wanted him.

Miss Akin was obviously surprised to see Kade. Her eyes widened. "Good afternoon."

"Miss A, this is Kade. Kade, this is Miss A."

"I've never officially met you. It's a pleasure," she said, looking from Kade then back to me, her brows slightly furrowed. She looked a little concerned. Apparently it was different for me to be hanging out with Ian, a ghost she couldn't see, compared to a flesh-and-blood guy.

"It's nice to meet you, Miss A, is it?"

Miss A managed a tight-lipped smile. "Miss Akin, but the kids like to call me Miss A."

And she loved the nickname.

Kade nodded. "So—do you need help with bringing in the groceries?"

"Aye, indeed I do." She started back toward the door.

"No, Miss A…I'll get it."

He walked out the back door toward the car, and I smiled inwardly. He could pour on the charm and it seemed to be working… hook, line and sinker.

Miss A's brows rose to her hairline. "Oh my…he's a looker, isn't he?"

I laughed under my breath. I couldn't help it. God, I was so happy. "Yes, he definitely is."

"I didn't know you were having company today, else I would have baked something special."

Kade came in with four bags that he set on the counter, and Miss A fell silent. He glanced at me with a soft smile and my heart swelled.

He went back for more and Miss Akin watched his every step, her gaze fastening on his high, firm butt.

"Miss A," I said in a teasing tone.

She lightly slapped her cheek. "My goodness, I'm sorry. Here I am ogling your friend. I just can't help but admire the view. So tall... and strapping."

He was both those things.

I slipped away upstairs to blow-dry my hair, put on some mascara, blush and lip gloss, as well as a cute knit shrug that fell just beyond my elbow. The scratches on my arm and back had faded, but I still felt self-conscious about the scars.

The more time I spent with Kade, the more I liked him. I would have expected him to be a player like Johan, but he wasn't. He had an irresistible charm.

Kade forgot to bring a movie. Rather than watch a chick flick from my mom's collection, which is all I had, we watched *Braveheart*, compliments of Miss A who sat down in her rocking chair and watched with us.

She seemed terrified to leave us alone together for more than a stretch of ten minutes. Every single time she got up, Kade reached over and kissed me. Those kisses, and his touch alone made the hair on my arms stand on end.

"What about some shortbread cookies," Miss Akin asked, looking specifically at Kade.

"I love shortbread cookies," he said.

She beamed, popped out of her chair and rushed toward the kitchen.

Kade slid his arm across the back of the couch.

I slid my head against his shoulder, and his arm immediately tightened around me. It felt really good to be in his strong arms. For a short time it was nice not to think about Laria.

The front door opened and closed. I expected it to be Shane, and was shocked when my Dad walked by. Seeing me, he stopped short, his brows furrowed as he looked from me to Kade.

Talk about horrible timing.

I stood up and Kade did too. "Hey, Dad. This is my friend Kade MacKinnon."

Kade walked over to my dad and extended his hand. "Mr. Williams, it's nice to meet you."

"Nice to meet you, Kade." Dad shook his hand and looked at me. "Is Shane here?"

"No, but he'll be home soon."

Dad smiled tightly. "I'll be in my study until dinner." He turned back to Kade. "Miss Akin said your family had Riley over for dinner. I'd like to return the favor. Would you stay for dinner?"

Dinner at my house was the polar opposite of dinner at Kade's house. We sat in the sparse dining room as a family for the first time, instead of sitting at the breakfast bar, or everyone taking their plates to their rooms. Kade sat to my right, Shane across from us, Miss Akin at one end, and my dad at the other.

It was a good thing Shane sat across from me since I suspected he was blazed. His eyes weren't red, but they were glassy. He was quiet, replying in one word responses to every question Dad directed at him. Within ten minutes he'd inhaled two plates of lasagna and four bread sticks.

Conversation was awkward at best. Dad seemed distracted and his cell phone went off a couple of times. Finally, he grabbed it from his pocket.

Oh my God, was he actually texting?

Shane laughed under his breath, but pressed his lips in a thin line when Dad frowned at him.

My only saving grace was Miss Akin who kept the mood upbeat, and conversation flowing, even if she was the one doing most of the talking. She brought in a plate of shortbread cookies for dessert. Shane grabbed a handful. "It's been nice, but I have some homework to finish."

Yeah right.

Dad pushed back from the table. "Oh, hey before you go, I'm headed out to London tomorrow for a few days. How much money do you need for the week?" Dad asked, already pulling out his wallet.

He was leaving again? Was Shane right? Was Dad seeing someone?

Shane held out his hand. "Whatever you're willing to part with."

Dad smiled, shoved some bills in Shane's hand and ruffled his hair, his awkward attempt at showing affection. It was almost painful to watch.

Kade glanced at me and smiled, but I recognized the sympathy there.

It wasn't hard to tell that my family put the D in dysfunction.

"See you at practice tomorrow," Shane said to Kade.

"Sounds good," Kade replied, wiping his mouth with his napkin and setting it on his empty plate.

Dad placed a few bills in front of me. "I'll leave Miss Akin the credit card."

"Thanks," I murmured.

Sliding his wallet back into his pocket, Dad sat down and asked Kade a few questions, two of which he'd already asked before dinner. I was relieved when he finished his tea and then excused himself, saying he had business calls to make.

"I should get going," Kade said, stealing a few cookies off the plate. "Delicious, Miss A. Riley wasn't kidding when she said you were an excellent cook."

Her eyes lit up.

I walked Kade to the front door.

My dad's office door was open, and I heard him typing away on his computer.

"I had a great time. Thanks for having me," Kade said.

I rolled my eyes. "You're being nice."

"No, I really did." He gave me a hug. "You have a nice family."

"It was nice to meet you, Kade," my dad called from his study.

Kade's eyes widened. "You too, Mr. Williams." He kissed me softly. "That would be my cue to leave."

The day had been perfect. No interruptions from Laria, and aside from the awkward dinner, Kade seemed to like my family, which was important to me. Even more, my family liked him.

I waited at the door until Kade got in his car and pulled out of the driveway.

"He's a nice young man."

Dad stood at his study doorway.

"Kade is nice. You'd like his family, too." I was relieved he liked him. "Mr. MacKinnon said he'd like to have you over sometime."

"That's very nice. I'll have to take him up on the offer one day soon...when things aren't so hectic with work." He shifted on his feet. "Did your mom ever talk to you about protection?"

Oh my God. Talk about awkward.

"I mean, you're at that age, and I thought that maybe, I mean—considering you have a boyfriend." His gaze dropped to the floor between us.

"I've been on birth control pills since I was fourteen."

His eyes widened in horror.

I suppose it made sense that my mom had never mentioned me

being on the pill to my dad. What dad wants to hear that? "Because my periods were so irregular," I blurted, feeling my face turn warm. "It's common. A lot of girls are on the pill for the same reason."

"Well, okay then," he said, sounding relieved. "Good night."

"Good night, Dad. It's good to have you home."

Chapter Fifteen

I awoke to voices coming from Shane's room.

Had one of Shane's friends dropped by last night after I'd crashed? A screeching noise sounded, like furniture being dragged slowly across the floor. I sat up, listening intently.

The voices continued. A strange whispering, and I swore to God I heard a girl's voice.

Was Joni here?

I rested my ear against the wall.

A horrible sound came from the other side—like a growl that sent shivers down my spine. I couldn't understand what had been said...but it wasn't good.

Reaching for my robe, I threw it on, and taking a deep, steadying breath, left my room and walked to Shane's bedroom door. I considered knocking, but instead opened the door.

I smothered a scream.

Shane was levitating a few feet off the bed—his body stick straight, his shaggy hair falling away from him.

"Shane," I said, taking a step closer. Without looking away from my brother, I felt for the light switch and turned it on.

The bulb flashed and went out.

A lava lamp was the only light in the room, casting the room in a bluish glow. Behind me, the door creaked shut. I swallowed hard and took a step closer. "Shane."

Once again, nothing.

The window was open, the drapes fluttering softly in the breeze. Shane never slept with his window open. I knew that for a fact. His whole life he'd always been terrified of the dark and paranoid about the boogieman, even climbing into bed with me. There's no way he'd open the window. No frickin' way.

My brother's body started moving from a horizontal position to a vertical one; slowly, inch by inch he floated up toward the ceiling.

I was frozen with fear. I didn't know what to do. "Shane, please wake up. Please..."

When his head bumped the ceiling, his neck began to bend in a strange, unnatural, and yet all too familiar angle.

Laria. How many times had she appeared to me in that same, broken neck position?

Shane's eyes snapped open. The usual blue orbs were dark brown and fathomless as he stared at me without blinking.

"Shane," I said, jumping onto the bed, grabbing his legs and trying to pull him down, but he only choked harder. My efforts seemed to be making matters worse.

He flinched, blinked, and started choking and even reached for his neck. Terrified, I ran down the hall toward my dad's room and opened the door. "Dad, help! Shane's choking."

"What?" he said, already out of bed.

I ran back toward Shane's room and stopped in my tracks. Dad ran into my back.

Shane stood in the hallway right outside his room, and he was facing me with a blank expression.

"Shane, are you okay?" Dad asked.

Shane's gaze flicked to Dad. "Of course I'm okay."

"But you were—" The words died on my lips.

His head tilted slightly and his eyes narrowed as he looked at me once more. I clamped my lips together. There was a strange expression on his face, one that let me know it most likely wasn't my brother staring back at me.

"Is everything all right?" Miss A asked from the far end of the hall.

"Yes, everything is fine, Miss Akin," Dad said, scrubbing his stubble. "Go back to bed. We're sorry to have disturbed you."

She nodded and went back into her room and shut the door.

"Sorry, I thought I heard Shane choking," I said. "I went into his room and he couldn't stop, so I panicked."

Dad gave an exaggerated sigh. "Well, he's fine now. Aren't you, Shane?"

Shane glanced at Dad. "Yes, I'm fine."

"There, you see...your brother is fine, Riley. Now get back to bed. You have school in the morning."

Settling back into bed under my dad's watchful gaze, I tried to calm down. Laria's threats came back to taunt me. She was doing whatever she could to get to me, and now she was using Shane. I knew that without a doubt. I lay on my side, facing the door.

On the other side of the wall, I heard whispers again and I placed the pillow over my head.

"Riiiiiileeeeeey." The voice itself was hair raising, a deep-throated growl that made me want to cry.

Over the growl, I heard a woman's laughter.

The following day at school I couldn't focus on anything. All I could think about was the look on Shane's face when he'd been levitating. It's like he had been completely possessed. I'd never even watched a horror movie that dealt with possession. The idea that someone could be taken over by an entity had been too scary.

After first period I walked into the bathroom, and knew something was up when I walked out of the stall to find Joni crying. Mascara ran down her face, and her girlfriends rallied around her.

Seeing me, they fell silent.

"Are you okay?" I asked, turning on the faucet and washing my hands.

Joni's friend, a stocky girl with frizzy dark hair and freckles put her hands on her hips and lifted a brow. "Your brother is an asshole."

I opened my mouth, ready to defend Shane when Joni shook her head. "It's not Riley's fault. Don't take it out on her."

I hadn't really gotten to know Joni, and now I was kind of glad I hadn't. I didn't need to get involved in my brother's love life. "For what it's worth—I'm sorry," I said, before walking out in the hallway.

In the distance I saw Shane talking up a cute brunette.

He definitely didn't waste any time. No wonder Joni was so upset. This is one of those times I wished my mom was still alive, or that my father actually gave a shit about what was happening in our lives.

But the hard truth was...my mom was dead and my dad may as well be for all that he cared about the two of us. If it wasn't for Miss Akin we would be on our own.

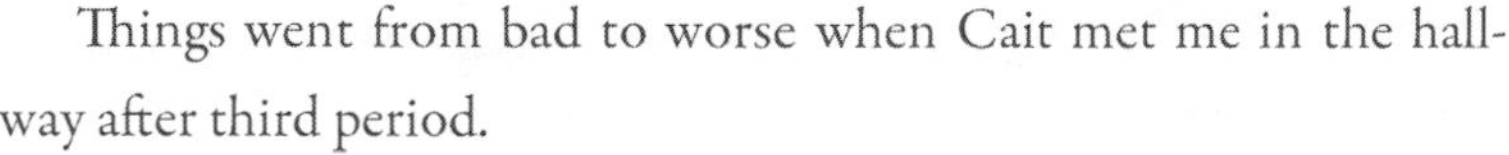

Things went from bad to worse when Cait met me in the hallway after third period.

"Your brother completely lost his shit in Mr. Cameron's class today."

Alarm rushed through me. "What happened?"

"He called Mr. Cameron a prick and tossed the exam paper back in his face. He almost punched him but Richie stepped in. Rumor has it he's been suspended for three days."

Shane might be a smart-ass, but he usually always respected teachers and had never been in any kind of trouble before. Well, aside from hitting a teammate for talking shit about his girlfriend.

Nor had he levitated.

I couldn't walk ten feet down the hallway without someone mentioning Shane.

At lunch, I went straight to the library. I breathed a sigh of relief to see only one other person on the computer. I took a seat at the table furthest away from everyone and typed *signs of spirit possession* into the search engine.

Sweat formed on my forehead as site after site said similar things and gave a list of symptoms that implied a person had been taken over by a spirit. Shane had the majority of the signs, but then again, so did I...and so did Anne Marie. I remembered Shane telling me before Ian had left that he'd been having strange dreams and felt a heaviness around him, which went along with spirit possession.

I continued reading.

Over and over again I read that spirits normally were attracted to sensitive individuals, particularly those who were weak—meaning physically weak, like those who were sick or had lowered immune systems, or those who were spiritually weak.

I didn't consider my brother weak by any means, but he was sensitive to spirits. He had felt Laria, even if he'd been unable to see her. Hell, he hadn't even slept at the inn for days on end because of strange dreams he'd been having. I thought of Anne Marie who had suffered through the same thing. Laria had found a way to literally get inside Shane. Had she done the same to Anne Marie? Is that why Anne Marie had left town so abruptly?

"Whatcha doing?"

I jumped a foot and put a hand to my racing heart. "You scared me."

Peter stood beside me, looking all wide-eyed and innocent.

"Sorry," he said, not sounding at all sorry. He leaned forward and squinted at the screen. "Signs of spirit possession, huh?"

"Homework," I replied.

"Liar," he said under his breath, a smile on his lips.

A girl at another table glanced over at me, her brows furrowed together, reminding me that I was now talking to myself. I needed to speak with Peter telepathically.

"Can you take over a living person?"

His brows furrowed. *"What do you mean, exactly?"*

"Like possess someone. Manipulate their thoughts and their bodies."

"Why do you ask?"

"Because I think my brother is being possessed by Laria."

Maybe it was my imagination, but Peter didn't look at all surprised.

Sliding into the chair next to me, he leaned close. *"I know that some living people have taken on the personality of a spirit. There are a lot of us in spirit who are trying to communicate. We're pushing thoughts and feelings toward the living, hoping to receive some kind of response."*

"How can a person keep a spirit from taking them over?"

"They can't really. I mean, for whatever reason the person is open to it—whether they know it or not. There's protection, but only that works so much."

Hardly encouraging. I personally knew how strong Laria was. She terrified me with her strength and her ability to shift personas. She had warned me before that she would hurt those I loved, and I had no doubt that she was doing exactly that. If she couldn't get in me, she'd get inside my brother.

"How can I stop her?"

He chewed on his lower lip and shrugged. *"I don't know. She's very powerful."*

I was disappointed. I needed help and real answers. I ran my hands down my face. I needed to talk to Anne Marie. I needed to talk to someone, and someone living. Someone that had interactions with ghosts like me. Madison immediately came to mind, and yet I didn't exactly feel comfortable pulling a twelve-year-old girl into my living nightmare.

But Madison knew Laria. She had told me as much herself. And what about Hanway? Would he talk to me? I wondered. Could he give me insight and tell me how to fight Laria...or were they friends?

"I don't know if Hanway will speak. He never leaves the castle. You'd have to go to him." I looked up at Peter in surprise. I forgot that oftentimes ghosts could read our thoughts.

"Why don't you go to the castle?" I asked, since the question had been eating at me for awhile.

He shrugged and looked down. *"There are areas in Braemar I don't dare go, one place being the castle. There are spirits—who are not good. They are cruel, not only to the living but to the dead as well. So I stay where I am comfortable."*

"Is there more than one mean spirit in the castle?" I thought of Randall Cummins.

"There are mean spirits everywhere...just as there are mean people everywhere. A person doesn't change who they are when they die. If an earthbound spirit was cruel in life, then that spirit would be cruel in death."

That made sense to me. *"Will you always stay here...I mean in the school?"*

"I don't know."

One day I hoped I could talk Peter into passing over into the light. Even though he seemed happy, I wanted him to pass on.

"If you don't mind me asking—how did you die?"

"Tuberculosis."

"That affects the lungs, right?"

Peter glanced up toward the door. *"Uh-oh."*

Kade walked into the library. He scanned the room, and seeing me he grinned.

I hit the computer's *Off* button and closed my notebook. I didn't want to have to explain to Kade why I was searching about spirit possession.

"There you are," Kade said, glancing at the computer.

"I thought I'd get a jump on homework. I've been slammed lately and the last thing I need is bad grades." I ran a hand through my hair, and twisted the ends around my finger.

"I thought maybe you were ignoring me," he said jokingly, but I could see a certain vulnerability in his eyes that surprised me.

"Of course I'm not ignoring you. I had fun this weekend," I said, and immediately he seemed to relax.

"I did, too. In fact, I was hoping maybe we could get together tonight...after practice." I could tell by his body language that he was nervous. "Do you want to come to my house for dinner? We can have Shane and Miss A over too."

How sweet of him to think of Miss A and Shane. Honestly, given what was going on with Shane, it probably wasn't the best time to accept the family invite.

"I'd love to come to dinner."

He actually breathed a sigh. "I'll pick you up at 6:30."

"All right," I replied, happy he'd asked. I wanted to spend time with him, and I was grateful for the chance to go to his house, and hopefully talk to Madison.

He helped me to my feet, his fingers sliding through mine. We walked toward the door hand in hand. My heart raced as we walked out into the hallway. I could see people watching us, the surprise on their faces. Kade glanced at me, a soft smile on his lips.

I guess this meant we were officially together.

Dana's friend was standing at her locker. Seeing us, she dropped a book. She picked it up and rushed down the hallway, no doubt to tell Dana.

"I had a dream about you last night," he said softly.

I tensed. "I'm almost afraid to ask if it was good or bad."

"Mostly weird," he said with a strained laugh that didn't exactly put me at ease. "We were in the castle, searching and rummaging through boxes."

My heart skipped a beat. "What were we looking for?"

"A book."

"A book?" I repeated, excitement rushing up my spine.

"Yes, we finally found it...in a chest. The chest my mom keeps in her study, or what we like to call the catch-all."

"What did we do with the book?" I asked.

"You have it in your room," he said matter-of-factly. "Hidden away."

Adrenaline coursed through my veins. This was just further proof to me that Kade *was* Ian. He had to be. How else could he know about that night in the castle and about Laria's journal?

When I didn't say anything, he cleared his throat. "Completely mental, right?"

I could have kissed him, but instead I squeezed his hand. "Not at all. Dreams can be hard to interpret," I said, wishing I could tell him about Ian without making myself sound crazy.

Dana walked by us, her lips quirked as her gaze dropped to our linked hands. "Hey, Kade." She gave me a lethal stare.

"Hey," he said, his thumb brushing over mine, reassuring me in his own way.

I smiled at him, and missed a step when I saw Laria standing directly between me and the door to my classroom. Thank God I was holding hands with Kade.

Her appearance was more frightening to me—her eyes more sunken in than I remembered, the almost purple circles more pronounced, making her dark eyes appear black.

"You're trembling," Kade said, his expression concerned.

Cold air enveloped me, chills working their way up my legs and arms. I wanted to run in the opposite direction.

Laria reached out for me, her fingers running down my arm... directly over the now nearly healed scratches. I bit back a cry. It felt like someone poured alcohol over the cut. I winced against the pain and mentally repeated the words, *you have no power over me, you have no power over me, you have no power over me.*

She laughed cruelly, her face inches from mine, moving backward without taking a step. "I'm fine," I said to Kade.

"You sure?"

I nodded. "I'm sure."

I brushed a hand over my face. Laria vanished, and I sighed in relief.

We stopped at the classroom door. "I'll see you tonight, okay?"

"Sounds good," I replied, dropping his hand. I watched as he walked in long strides down the hall. Dread filled me seeing Laria at the very end of the hall. Kade was walking straight toward her.

My heart hammered in my chest. Oh my God, was she going after Kade now?

Kade glanced back over his shoulder, looked at me and lifted his hand.

I waved back.

"Miss Williams?" The teacher watched me, brows lifted. "The bell is about to ring. Please take your seat."

I looked one last time down the hallway...to find it empty.

Chapter Sixteen

The castle was quiet, surprising since every member of the MacKinnon household was home. It reminded me of the inn in a way—so large that a person could move around without anyone else hearing.

I sat beside Kade on his bed, his foot sliding against mine. His mom said she'd come get us when dinner was ready. She didn't seem to have a problem with us being in Kade's room alone...as long as we kept the door open. I had to smile at that, because my mom would have been exactly the same way.

I wondered if Kade knew how lucky he was to have her; to have a stable home life with parents who were attentive and who put their kids first.

His fingers brushed lazily along my thigh, up and down, sending the best kind of shiver through me. Aside from Miss Akin, he was the bright spot in my world, my comfort and shoulder to lean on. And I was falling hard...

He went in for a bone-melting kiss that had my heart pounding so loud I was sure he could hear it. And he was an incredible kisser. Soft lips. Perfect pressure, and I loved the way his hands always cupped my face. He made me feel fragile and cherished.

Footsteps sounded on the spiral steps, and as they drew closer, Kade sighed and put some distance between us.

"I made cookies," his mom said, popping her head in. I could tell by her expression that she wasn't exactly comfortable with me being on her son's bed, and I felt my cheeks turn warm as she placed the plate on top of the dresser. "Now don't eat too many. I don't want you to spoil your dinner."

Feeling awkward, I stood up and sampled a cookie. "Excellent," I said, even though the cookies were definitely dry and had a strange baking soda aftertaste to them. No wonder Kade had devoured Miss A's shortbread cookies.

She beamed. "I'm so glad you like them. I'll package some up for you to take home to your family."

"Thanks. That's nice."

"Dinner will be ready shortly, so if you'd like, you can come to the dining room."

She wasn't asking us, she was telling us. I obediently followed her out the door. Behind me, Kade sighed heavily.

I glanced back over my shoulder and caught him staring at my butt. He gave me a sheepish smile.

"Hey, Riley," Madison said the second we entered the dining room. She sat in one of the chairs in front of the fireplace. She grinned, looking genuinely happy to see me.

"Hey you." I don't know why I expected Hanway to be hanging around, but when he wasn't, I was disappointed. I wished there was a way for me to talk to him about Laria.

Cait walked in, head down as she texted. She glanced up, and seeing me, she stopped short and smiled. "Hey Ri. When did you get here?"

"Riley is your brother's guest tonight," Karen said before I could respond.

"Ah, I see..." Cait flashed a cheeky grin and sat down at the table, patting the chair next to her and telling me to sit.

The second Mrs. MacKinnon left the room, Cait said, "So what's the deal with your brother? Last I heard he broke things off with Joni?"

Wow, word traveled fast.

"I haven't had a chance to talk to him, but I do know he's going through a rough time right now."

Madison watched us closely, and she opened her mouth, but closed it a second later.

Cait took a sip of ice water, and set the glass back down. "So what did your dad say?"

"Nothing, he's out of town. I know Miss Akin will have to tell him about the suspension, and I dread when she does. I mean, it's been tough for Shane since my mom died."

"I'm sure it's been tough for both of you," Kade said, sitting across from me.

I nodded. "It has been, but we deal with stress in different ways."

I don't know if it was just my imagination, but I swore I saw Madison's gaze shift to my arm where the scratches were...the same arm where I had cut before. Since she spoke to spirits, had they told her my secret? Did they all know my secret? I wondered.

Mr. MacKinnon walked in and we all fell silent. Just like the last time I'd visited, he was warm and welcoming. During dinner, he talked about the time he'd taken Kade hunting and he bagged his first buck within the first hour. He was a natural with a bow, he had said with pride, and I remembered how Ian had told me he'd loved to hunt. I suppose it made sense that if we had a hobby in one life, that we would carry that hobby to the next life.

When I glanced at Kade, the sides of his mouth curved. "He exaggerates."

"I don't exaggerate. The boy is a natural, I tell you." Duncan dropped a few spoonfuls of sugar into his tea. "And fishing. He puts everyone else I know to shame. Our lucky charm, my friend Richard calls him."

"Everything Kade touches turns to gold," Cait said sarcastically, although she was smiling.

That's when I heard the chanting begin.

My insides clenched. Oh my God, not now. Not here.

"Riley." My name had been whispered in my ear. I sat up straighter, pressed the napkin to my lips and tried to get my racing heartbeat to slow down.

"Riley." It was clearer this time, and deeper, like a growl.

I glanced at Madison, whose face had gone ashen.

Did she hear it, too?

Cold air surrounded me, the hair on my arms standing on end.

I felt the spirit behind me, could feel the pressure of someone there. Across the room there was an intricate mirror on the wall. It was at eye level, so I couldn't see myself, but I could see someone standing behind me. Someone wearing a black cloak, a cowl covering their head, the features of their face hidden in shadow.

Hands settled on my shoulders. My gaze dropped to Madison and she was looking up—at someone behind me. I swallowed hard and our eyes met.

I intentionally knocked my water over onto my lap. "I'm so sorry. I'll go to the restroom," I said, standing abruptly.

"I'll show you where it's at," Madison said right behind me.

Cait frowned at her. "Seriously, Maddy. She—"

"No, that's fine," I said, my voice almost snappy. "I forgot where it was."

We said nothing to each other until we reached the bathroom. I stepped in and shut the door behind us.

"You saw it too?" I said.

She looked on the verge of tears. "What do they want?"

"I don't know. Did you see who it was?"

She shook her head. "No, the hood thingy hid the face. I'm scared, Riley." She took the step that separated us and buried her face against my shoulder.

"He's not after you," I said reassuringly, hugging her close.

"Hanway," Madison said, her eyes screwed tight. "Hanway, help."

Within seconds the tall Scot was standing before us.

I was so relieved to see him, and so was Madison who released a sigh.

Now that I had a chance to stare at him, he wasn't at all scary... just big. Massive, really.

"He's gone, lass," he said reassuringly, putting a hand on Madison's shoulder.

She rested her hand over his, and I couldn't help but smile. Hanway was what Ian had been to me.

"He won't be troubling you any longer. I'll see to it." He looked at me. "You are haunted by some black souls, my dear."

Souls as in plural.

"You said it was a man. Who is he?"

"Friends and allies of the one who seeks to destroy you."

I didn't want to say Randall Cummins' name aloud. "The servant in the picture?"

Hanway nodded. "Aye, the very man who introduced Laria to

the dark arts."

I shifted on my feet, wondering if I should ask questions in front of a twelve-year-old. I weighed my options and knew I had no choice but to go for it. I didn't know when next I would have the opportunity. "Can the dead take over a living person—like literally become that person?"

"Of course," he said, sounding like the question was ridiculous. "Especially the weak."

There it was again, that reference to weakness. Shane didn't seem weak to me.

"A person does not have to be physically or emotionally weak to be a target for the dead. Sometimes believing in nothing is the perfect invitation to a spirit to prove that there is another dimension beyond what that person believes in." He watched me closely. "And when a spirit wants revenge—he or she will look to those closest to the person they wish to harm."

"So are spirits able to take over a person's body for long periods of time?"

"Aye, if they are strong enough. But remember—even the most powerful among us must find energy in order to possess another."

Which explained why sometimes Shane seemed fine, and other times he didn't.

I knew very well how strong Laria's power was. And she had friends helping her, witches that were as dangerous and frightening as she was.

"If she could take you over, she would. You must remain strong, lass. Do not let her see your fear and always protect yourself."

Easier said than done, I thought.

Footsteps approached. "Cait comes," Hanway said.

Madison grabbed a hairdryer out of the drawer and handed it to me.

"Did you fall in?" Cait asked, trying the door.

Hanway held the knob firm. "You'll be all right, lass. Be strong."

He faded, and I was sorry to see him go. I had a million other questions for him.

Madison looked up at me, and I could see the fear in her eyes. She was scared for me. Actually, I was scared for myself.

The house was silent when I got home from Kade's house.

Clutching the bag of cookies Karen had sent me home with, I rounded the corner into the kitchen, turned on the light and stopped dead in my tracks.

Shane sat on a barstool.

He'd been sitting in the dark?

"Hey, what are you doing?"

He blinked a few times and frowned at the counter, before finally making eye contact with me. "I don't know." Dark circles bracketed his eyes and he looked exhausted.

"I heard about you getting suspended," I said, wondering exactly when he had come home.

There was no expression on his face as he watched me. I set the cookies on the counter. I remembered what Hanway had said about ghosts being able to manifest for certain lengths of time. Who exactly was Shane right now?

I noticed Shane's hands were trembling. I also noticed his eyes seemed darker than they'd been seconds before. Almost a slate color. Not a good sign.

"When did Miss A go to bed?" I asked, going to the fridge and pulling out juice. "You want a glass?"

Once again he just stared. I poured a glass of juice and set the decanter back in the fridge. I could feel Shane watching me, and even more, I felt hatred come off of him in waves. It was strange to be terrified of your own brother.

I turned and he was right behind me. I gripped the glass tight. I hadn't even heard him move. "Did you want juice?"

He stared at me, not blinking, his face inches from mine. "He will hurt you and when he does, you will wish you were dead."

"Why would you say that?"

The sides of his mouth curved into a slow, cruel smile. "Because it's the truth."

Shane walked away before I could reply.

I had to end this. I had to find a way to get my brother back. I had to keep reminding myself that I had brought Laria into our lives.

I just had to fix it. No matter what it took. Shane was being robbed of his life and manipulated by pure evil.

I looked in the address book that Miss Akin kept in a drawer in the kitchen and I dialed Anne Marie's cell number.

The phone rang four times before she picked up. "Hello."

"Anne Marie, it's Riley."

There was silence on the other end...for a second. "How are you?"

"Anne Marie?" Nothing but dial tone.

I dialed the number again and it immediately went to voice message. I waited a few minutes, and when my phone didn't ring again, I tried one more time. The phone rang this time. I put the address book away and Anne Marie answered. "Riley?"

"Yes, it's me."

"My dear, you are in gr—"

I could hear nothing but static on the line. "Anne Marie." I stayed on for another minute and hung up, my heart pounding out of my chest. Her voice had been intense, like she was warning me.

I went upstairs to my room and hit *Redial* again. Anne Marie picked up almost immediately, but after she said hello, the line once again went static.

Chapter Seventeen

Something was wrong—I could feel it in my bones. I'd grown accustomed to the smell of a five star breakfast. Today there was silence in the kitchen, and there were no signs or smells that Miss Akin had been there. Not even a cereal bowl. "Hello," I said, and my greeting was met with silence.

I rushed through the house, and finally raced up the steps and walked down the hallway toward Miss Akin's room, trying to ignore the sense of foreboding that was quickly overtaking me. I knocked on her door, and I heard shuffling inside.

"Please be okay," I whispered. I couldn't fathom losing her.

"Come in, dear."

Hearing her voice, I breathed a sigh of relief and opened the door.

Miss A sat on the edge of her bed holding a tissue, her shoulders slumped.

"Miss A, what's wrong?"

She glanced up. Her glasses sat on the nightstand, and she reached for them while she dabbed at her eyes. It tore at my insides to see her in pain, and I was actually terrified to learn what had made her so upset. I immediately thought of my dad. Had something happened to him?

"What's wrong?" I asked, steeling myself for the worst.

"I received some distressing news."

I took the steps that separated us, sat down beside her. "What is it?"

Her throat convulsed as she swallowed. "Anne Marie passed away this morning."

"But I just called her last night."

Miss Akin's eyes widened. "Did you speak with her?"

"Just for a second. There was too much static on the line." I didn't like where my thoughts were headed. Anne Marie had sounded like she was trying to warn me about something, and now she was dead. Was there a connection?

"What happened, Miss A?"

She picked at the edges of the tissue. "Her family isn't sure. She told them she wasn't feeling well last night and she went to bed and never woke."

I put an arm around her, rested my head on her shoulder. "I'm sorry, Miss A."

"That's not all. Last night I dreamt about her death. She stood right here—right there in this room," she said, nodding toward the end of the bed.

Miss A had told me about her precognitive dreams before. She'd often seen events before they happened. "What did she say?"

"She just smiled and said she was at peace, and then told me to protect you...and Shane. There was a sense of urgency. I kept asking her what she meant, and all she did was smile. When I awoke, I knew she was dead. I felt her absence. I know it sounds strange..."

"No, it doesn't."

She shook her head and started crying all over again. I felt horrible for her. Anne Marie was Miss Akin's closest friend. I knew too well the feeling of having someone you care about die. A piece of you dies with them.

"Look at me making such a fuss. She would hate that."

"You're allowed to cry, Miss A."

She turned to me, her gaze searching my face. "Are you all right, my darling? I mean, is there something or someone who is bothering you or your brother that I should know about?"

I couldn't bring myself to tell her about Laria and my suspicions about what she was doing to Shane. Especially now that Anne Marie was dead. "No, I'm doing better than I've been in a long time." At least it wasn't a total lie. "Listen, I'll stay home with you today."

"No, you need to go to school."

I would never be able to focus on my classes.

"Plus, Anne Marie's daughter Gretchen asked me to drop in if I was able. I think I might do just that. It's a forty-five minute drive, but it might do me good."

"I think that's a great idea." I knew how close Miss Akin and Anne Marie had been.

I wished there was something I could do or say to make her feel better.

"You sure you'll be okay for the day?"

She nodded, and as I walked out of the room, a wave of guilt assailed me. Had Anne Marie died because of me? She hadn't been acting like herself since the séance with Laria, and now she was dead. It was tough to ignore all the signs.

"You're all the talk of the school today," Cassandra said, appearing beside my locker the second I walked into school. I'd had calls from her and Meg last night, but I didn't have the chance to call back with the drama that was my life.

"School hasn't even started."

Her brows lifted. "Exactly. You should hear Dana. She's so jealous, she can hardly stand it." Cassandra giggled. "I love it."

Dana was the least of my worries. Megan joined us in the hall, and she was grinning from ear to ear. "Congratulations are in order, I hear." She whistled softly. "Kade MacKinnon. Someone has finally got to that boy. Leave it to the American to snag him. Kudos to you, my friend."

"Thanks," I said glumly, Anne Marie and Miss Akin still heavy on my mind.

"Why so down?" Cassandra asked.

"Miss A's best friend died last night."

"Sorry," they said in unison.

The double doors at the end of the locker bay opened and Kade walked in, flanked by Johan and Tom. Seeing me, he smiled, and I felt the familiar butterflies flutter in my belly whenever I was around him.

Cassandra laughed. "Look at you, you're beaming."

I doubted that I was beaming, but I was happy to see him. I wanted to run into his arms and have him tell me everything would be fine.

Megan watched Kade's approach with a smug smile. "I knew it," she said mostly to Cassandra. "Didn't I tell you he was totally into her?"

Cassandra nodded, her gaze shifting to Johan. By the hot look they shared, I had little doubt they were hooking up again.

Kade walked right up to me and pulled me in for a kiss. "Good morning."

"Morning," I said, wanting to tell him about Anne Marie, but not when we had an audience.

Johan and Tom both looked surprised about the PDA. Not so for Milo who came up from behind the boys and put an arm around Megan's neck. "Morning, love," he whispered against the side of her head.

"Mornin', Megan replied."

Milo glanced at me. "Ri." His gaze shifted to Kade and he winked.

"Milo," I said.

At least Megan seemed to be back to her old self. I still found it odd she had never mentioned a word about the ride home from Aberdeen.

Cassandra's gaze lingered on Johan. "See you at lunch," she said absently.

Kade's fingers slid through mine. "Walk you to class?"

"Sure." My heart squeezed as I looked into his blue eyes. I was falling hard.

"I have practice after school. Can I drop by the inn after?"

"Sure, but just for a little while. Miss A's best friend died last night."

He shot me a concerned look. "I'm so sorry. Who was her friend?"

"Anne Marie."

His brow furrowed. "Older lady with the purple tint to her hair?"

I nodded.

"Well, maybe I'll just drop by for a few minutes."

"Okay."

We parted ways at my classroom.

I took my seat and noticed immediately that people were talking. No big surprise. The new girl had snagged the football star. I'm sure I would have a bull's-eye on my forehead.

Speaking of—Dana straightened when she saw me, her gaze shifting over me, taking in every detail while shaking her head.

"He just wants to take her virginity before anyone else does," she said to the friend next to her.

I bit the inside of my lip.

Is that what everyone thought? That Kade wanted me only because of my virginity? It couldn't be that he actually liked me or that we had a connection.

The teacher wrote our assignment on the board, and I was glad that we would have forty-five minutes to read to ourselves. It would be tough to focus on what I was reading, and not think about anything but the assignment.

I cracked my book open and started reading the first page. The text was boring, but I forced myself to focus and even took notes.

A loud screeching sound made me jump.

Standing at the chalkboard stood the man I had seen with Laria. The same man who had been in the visions; the man who had come to get her at the castle. Randall Cummins, the servant who Hanway said had introduced black magic to Laria.

I sat up straighter. He carried a sickle and tossed it from hand to hand, a sinister expression on his ugly face.

I looked around to see if anyone else noticed him. Everyone else was reading. Mr. Monahan glanced at me, frowned, and tapped his textbook.

I dropped my gaze to the book in front of me. The man with the sickle started walking toward me, the sickle falling on every desk along the way, making a horrible screeching sound. How could no one else hear that?

Cold chills raced up my arms and the closer he came to me, the more scared I became. I wanted to run, but was I really in danger in a classroom with twenty-five other students?

I set my pencil down on my notebook and gripped the edges of my book.

The ghost's fingers brushed against my hand, moving slowly up my arm. He leaned down, his lips inches from my ear. "So lovely. What a shame you must die."

I cringed as the backs of his fingers moved up along the inside of my elbow, my upper arm, my shoulder, his fingers brushing over my hair. "So sweet." He leaned down, his face next to the top of my head. He inhaled deeply. "Like fresh fruit."

"Stop, witch!"

The ghost vanished, as fast as he had come. My heartbeat was a roar in my ears. Anne Marie stood two feet away, so faint I could barely see her. But she was here, and she had managed to scare the other spirit away. I had a million questions to ask her, but she disappeared before I could blink.

Chapter Eighteen

An intense heaviness seemed to fall over the house the moment my dad walked through the door on Thursday afternoon.

"Shane," he yelled, and I braced myself for the worst. I had little doubt he'd received the less-than-good news about the trouble Shane had gotten himself into.

"He's at practice," I said, walking out of the parlor where I'd been watching television.

He frowned. "I thought he was suspended."

I wasn't touching this one with a ten-foot pole, but I had little choice but to say something since he was waiting for my answer. "Just for a few days."

"Just for a few days," he said, brows shooting to his hairline.

Miss Akin walked into the entry. "Welcome home, Mr. Williams."

"Thank you, Miss Akin." Setting his briefcase down, he gave her a hug. "I am so sorry about your friend."

"Thank you, sir."

Taking a step away, he glanced at me. "You look tired."

I didn't doubt it. I was exhausted from lack of sleep and my constant fear of Laria showing up when I least expected it. "I am."

"Get to bed early tonight," he said absently. "And let me know the second Shane gets home." Grabbing his briefcase, he headed upstairs to his room.

"Dinner is at six, my dear," Miss A said. "Why don't you take a nap before then."

I didn't argue with her, though I knew I wouldn't be able to nap.

I was in my room when Shane walked through the door. I heard him taking the steps two at a time, his room door opening and closing.

Seconds later Dad's footsteps sounded in the hallway.

The two were in a full-on yelling match by the time the doorbell rang. I hated to even answer it, but I wasn't about to leave Kade standing at the door. Every night this week he had dropped by after practice to see me. He'd brought Miss Akin flowers the other day after learning about Anne Marie's death.

"Is this a bad time?" he asked, his eyes widening upon hearing the yelling coming from the second floor.

I stepped outside and shut the door behind me. "Dad's home and he's heard about Shane's suspension."

"You okay?" he asked, pulling me in for a hug.

Sinking into him, I immediately relaxed, my arms sliding around his waist, my cheek on his chest. What I wouldn't give to go home with him and get away from the doom and gloom that had overtaken my home. I was beginning to hate it here.

"I'm fine. Maybe we can make it another night."

"You could always come over to my house, you know." His voice sounded hopeful.

"I wish I could come over, but I can't being my Dad just got home. Plus, I need to help Miss Akin with stuff for Anne Marie's memorial tomorrow."

"I understand," he said, kissing me softly.

I looked up into his handsome face. I wanted to be with him more than anything, but I needed to be here for Shane.

I heard a crash come from inside. "I should go."

"Do you want me to come with you?"

I shook my head. "Trust me, you don't want to get involved."

When another crash sounded, and I heard Shane call Dad an asshole, I stepped away from Kade. "I have to go."

"Call me later, okay?"

"I will." I watched until he got into his car before I walked back inside. Miss A stood in the hallway, looking hesitant to go upstairs.

"Why don't you go back to Edinburgh, or London, or wherever the hell it is you go every single week!" Shane yelled.

The door to Shane's room opened. He emerged, his eyes full of rage as he stormed downstairs.

Dad was right on his heels, but he stopped at the top of the stairs. "Get back here right now, young man. I'm not finished talking to you."

"I'm finished talking to you," Shane said under his breath, marching right past me like I wasn't there.

"Don't you dare walk out that door." Dad marched down the stairs.

Shane stopped for all of two seconds, his hand on the door handle.

"Don't do it, Shane." I hadn't realized I'd said the words aloud until he turned and glanced at me. I looked for signs of my brother in that stare.

He stared right through me and he walked out the door.

I was on the phone with Kade when Shane returned at midnight. Sitting on my bed, I could hear his footsteps as he climbed the steps, then the door to his room open and close. His music turned on low.

"I'll talk to you tomorrow," I told Kade, and set my phone on my nightstand.

Taking a deep breath, I walked to Shane's room.

I knocked.

"Come in."

At least he was answering me. A good sign.

He sat at the edge of his bed, face in hands.

"Are you okay?" I asked, putting a hand on his shoulder.

"I don't know. I feel like I'm losing my mind." He glanced up at me, and I breathed a sigh of relief seeing those familiar blue eyes.

Encouraged that he wanted to talk, I sat down beside him.

"What's wrong?"

"Milo and Richie tell me things I've been saying and doing...and I don't remember anything." He raked his hands through his blonde hair, his fingers twisting in the strands. "I mean nada. Nothing. It's like I'm blacking out and forgetting long periods of time. You should hear some of the shit they've told me that I've done."

"When did it start?"

He shrugged. "Around the time school started. There are some days I don't remember at all."

"And you're not smoking pot?"

"Not twenty-four/seven," he said, sounding exhausted. "Granted, I've binged here and there, but for the most part I haven't smoked. I don't get it. I feel like I'm losing it."

"I've noticed the change in you, too."

He glanced up. "Like what?"

I told him about all the times I'd seen him where he didn't seem like he'd been there, like the other night in the kitchen when he'd been sitting in the dark and the mean things he'd said to me. As expected, he didn't remember anything. I debated telling him about the levitation incident, and yet I needed to lay it on the line.

At first I could see disbelief in his eyes…which suddenly turned to something else.

"You will never be able to get rid of me." The deep voice wasn't Shane's.

The hair on the back of my neck stood on end, and I went to stand up, but he caught my wrist.

I swallowed hard.

"No one can save you. No one."

I knew that voice.

Even though I stared at my brother, I knew this was Laria. I sat up straight and tried to keep calm, which wasn't easy when Shane's nails were digging into my wrist. "Leave my brother alone, Laria."

"Leave my brother alone," he mimicked, his lips twisting into a cruel grin, before his head fell back on his shoulders and he laughed, a horrible sound that made my blood run cold. "You have no idea who you are up against. No idea…"

"You're wrong—I do know who I'm up against." I yanked my arm out of his grasp and stood. "I want my brother back."

Tears clogged my throat. With a calm that surprised me, I rushed for the door.

I don't know how he moved so fast without me hearing him. He yanked me back against his chest, his breath freezing cold against my ear. "I will kill *everyone* you love."

My gaze fastened on the bookcase where I saw a can of spray paint, red cap signaling Shane had been the one who had written CUTTER on my wall.

I elbowed him as hard as I could. He grunted and released me.

I ran for my room. Slamming my door shut, I grabbed a chair and slid it beneath my door handle. I wouldn't lie—I was more terrified than I'd ever been. Laria was slowly picking away at my resolve, and I was beginning to crumble.

"Mom, I need you...please," I whispered. I sat cross-legged on my bed facing the door, closed my eyes and did deep breathing. It took longer than usual, but I slowly calmed down. Although I hadn't prayed for a very long time, I did that as well. I even did a protection prayer I had found on the Internet, imagining a golden white light all around me.

At three in the morning I woke to the sound of footsteps outside my door. I had kept my light on, and I didn't move a muscle as I watched the knob slowly turn, and the chair budge a little. If it were Miss A or even my dad, they would say something.

Terrified, I hugged my pillow tight.

The knob moved a few more times, and I heard Shane say my name, but I couldn't bring myself to open it. I cried, horrified at what our lives had become—and all because of a vengeful spirit.

The bed squeaked when he got into bed. I waited fifteen minutes for anything to happen, for the creepiness to ensue. I didn't know if I expected to hear voices...but I heard nothing.

Chapter Nineteen

I noticed a change in Shane the next day. During Anne Marie's memorial service, he seemed more like his regular self. And at the potluck at Anne Marie's home afterward, he even chatted up one of Harry's granddaughters, a cute fourteen-year-old who blushed every time Shane walked by.

Karen had been at the service, and she dabbed at her eyes. Kade stayed by my side and held my hand. I appreciated him taking the time to attend the service, and when he asked me to take a drive with him after the potluck, I jumped at the chance.

Since Dad and Shane's fight, the house had been painfully quiet. Shane, who was grounded, spent his days in front of the television watching old karate movies and texting his friends. Dad would try to talk to him at dinner, but Shane didn't have much to say.

We said goodbye to everyone at Anne Marie's and Shane asked to catch a ride to the inn. I changed from the black dress into jeans, a tank and a plaid shirt that I rolled up to the elbow.

Kade rang the doorbell. I told Shane goodbye and opened the door. He'd changed into a well-worn T-shirt that did wonders for his eyes, and acid-washed jeans that hugged him in all the right places.

He reached out and took me by the hand. "You ready?"

We'd been driving for twenty minutes, and he'd just pulled off onto a long, tree-lined gravel drive. Kade glanced at me. "So...do you fish?"

"You're taking me fishing?" I asked, trying to hide my surprise. "Are you trying to impress me?"

"My dad did talk me up, didn't he?"

"Just a bit."

I'd been fishing a few times with my grandpa when I was little and remembered the thrill of catching a sturgeon on the Columbia River. Shane had said it was a baby shark that had swam from the Pacific Ocean into the river, and I'd been so terrified, I'd refused to go fishing again.

Exiting the car, I met Kade at the back of the Range Rover, where he took out the fishing poles and tackle box.

"It's a nice swimming hole, too," Kade said, placing the beat-up tackle box on the well-worn wood planks. "This is where both Cait and I learned to swim. My dad showed us the tough love method."

"'Tough love method?" I asked.

"He tossed us in and we had to sink or swim."

"Isn't that called child abuse?"

He laughed. "I suppose, but the technique worked. We both dog -paddled our way back to the dock. We swallowed a ton of water but we survived."

Kicking off his shoes, he then rolled up his pants. I did the same, sliding my feet into the cool water. Kade had a small container, and when he popped the lid, worms squiggled about. I wrinkled my nose and he laughed under his breath.

I had never had a problem with putting worms on the hook, and now was no exception. I surprised myself with how simple it was, remembering my grandpa's technique. Kade even looked impressed.

I stood up, swung the pole over my shoulder, cast out…and completely overshot the river.

So much for showing off.

Although Kade tried not to laugh, he did, and I laughed right along with him, especially when my line snagged the brush on the opposite side of the bank.

"Let me help you with that," he said, standing behind me, the front of his body flush against the back of mine. Warmth spread like wildfire through my veins.

I glanced over my shoulder at him, and he grinned, deep dimples and all.

He took the pole from my hand, and with a few sharp tugs, had the line free. He handed the rod back to me, and I immediately missed the contact.

I reeled in the line and tried casting again, this time hitting the river and letting the line float downstream a little before I started reeling in the slack.

"Nicely done," Kade said, a look of pride on his face.

I sat back down beside him, watching as he effortlessly cast his line into the center of the river, letting it drift down a ways before reeling in.

The sun came through the clouds and started to warm up fast. Despite the fact my feet were submerged in cold water, sweat beaded on my forehead. I started to take my shirt off but thought better of it.

"Take off your shirt. Take off both, if you like. Honestly, I won't mind." His smoldering grin heated my blood.

It seemed silly not to take off my shirt, especially when I was sweating. The scars from cutting were on the inside of my elbow, so I'd just have to be careful how I held my arm. And if he asked, then I'd just have to come clean, because I wasn't going to lie.

I slid the plaid shirt off and he helped. He set it behind us at the same time my pole jumped. I came to my feet and lifted up on the pole. I felt a snag, and hoped I had a fish on. I reeled it in, trying to keep my excitement at bay.

The fish wasn't large, but I was elated to be the first one to catch something. Kade grinned like crazy as he helped me take the slippery trout off the hook, which was one thing I had a tough time doing with it moving so much.

He carefully pulled the hook out of its mouth and tossed it back into the water a second later.

I frowned at him. "What did you do that for?"

"We're just catching and releasing."

"So you fish just for the sport of it?"

"Something like that," he said laughing.

I leaned my head against Kade's shoulder, forgetting about my pole until I heard it screech against the pier as the water dragged along.

Kade was quick, though. He reached down, snatched it from the water, and handed it back to me.

I baited the hook and cast again, and we both sat back down on the dock, his hand resting on my thigh.

"Maddy wanted to come today."

I smiled. "She cracks me up."

"She's a riot sometimes...but then she has moments where she's such a little shit."

"I suppose I understand why she's that way. She hasn't had the easiest life. She's lucky she has your family."

He nodded. "Honestly, there are times she gets on my nerves... but I try to remember myself at her age. And like you said, she hasn't had the easiest life."

"Seems like she gets on Cait's nerves, too."

"I think all siblings get on each other's nerves. I'm sure you and your brother do the same."

"Definitely."

"I think Cait likes your brother."

"I think Shane is having the time of his life being the new guy in town."

"And what about you, Riley—do you like being the new girl? Having every guy in school want you?" I could see the teasing glimmer in his eye...but I swore I recognized jealousy too.

What a strange thing to say. I didn't get the feeling that any one guy thought I was special. Aside from Johan, who had spent a little time with me this summer, no guys were knocking on my door or blowing up my phone.

"I'm not exactly the guy magnet you seem to think I am."

"You could have fooled me. Aaron Johnson can't keep his eyes off you, I understand."

Was the football star actually jealous of a band geek? The very thought made me smile inwardly.

He gave me a confidence I didn't realize I'd had before.

He kissed my forehead. "Aaron is a broken man now that you're taken."

I rolled my eyes. "Yeah, okay."

"I'm glad you came to Braemar, Riley," he said, his voice turning serious. "I'm glad you're here."

Once again he'd said the exact words Ian had said to me.

"I'm glad I'm here, too, and I'm glad I met you."

The afternoon sun started beating down on us, and Kade peeled his shirt off and then unbuttoned his pants.

"What are you doing?" I asked, my heart picking up speed as I checked out his six-pack abs, the deep V, and the dark happy trail, or what I'd heard Megan refer to as the "stairway to heaven" that disappeared into the waistband of his boxer briefs.

"It's too bloody hot to fish."

I rolled my eyes. "You just said that because I caught one and you didn't."

He picked me up and acted like he was going to toss me in the water. Instead, he kissed me and slowly set me back on my feet. We kissed for a long time, until he pulled away. "Let's get in the water."

His pants were off a second later, and he stood in his boxer briefs.

I wondered if he was going to go au natural, when he dove into the water.

I scanned the area to make sure we were alone, and I slid off my pants first, and then hurried with my shirt. Thankfully I wore my best black bra and hot pink boy-cut panties.

Kade came up for air just then. He flipped his hair back and my stomach clenched. He was so beautiful...high cheekbones, water spiking off long lashes, and beautiful blue eyes that smoldered. He didn't even pretend not to check me out...his gaze slowly gliding down my body.

I jumped in, the cold water stealing the breath from my lungs for a few seconds.

Kade swam toward me and I went into his arms as he pulled me close for a kiss. We swam for a while and I followed him to the river's edge. My legs slid around his waist and he moaned, his hands cupping my bottom. There was that dark, heavy-lidded look to his eyes that had the blood pumping hard through my veins.

I scanned the area. "What if someone sees us?"

"Did you notice the private property signs when we came in?"

I hadn't been paying any attention.

"My family owns this land. No one is allowed in but us."

"What if your family drops by?"

His fingers unhooked my bra. My pulse skittered. I'd never been naked in front of anyone before.

"Is this why you brought me here?" I asked, keeping my voice even.

The words stopped him cold. "No, I thought maybe we could tick off one of those never have I ever questions though."

My virginity? I thought, and then realized he was talking about skinny-dipping.

He reached down, and a second later he lifted his boxers in his hand and tossed them on the shore.

Kade lifted a brow.

Summoning every ounce of courage I had, I slid my bra and panties off and threw them toward the bank.

Chapter Twenty

We skinny-dipped for a while, until our skin was pruned. Kade stepped out of the water to the bank to get our underwear, and I know I shouldn't have stared but I couldn't help it.

No wonder he was so confident.

He flashed a smile as he waded back in, and tossed me my bra and undies.

"Follow me," he said, swimming toward a large, flat rock. He pulled himself up and put his hand out for me. It was the perfect size to catch some rays, just big enough for both of us. We lay on our backs, hand in hand, eyes closed. I couldn't remember the last time I felt so at peace.

Feeling like I was being watched, I cracked an eye open and found Kade watching me. The sides of his mouth lifted in a smile that made my blood turn warm.

I rolled onto my side, and rested my hand on his chest. The pulse in his neck fluttered. He lifted his head, kissed me, and slowly eased me onto my back, his strong body covering mine.

A hot ache rushed through my belly. My fingers splayed over the hard muscles of his back, and over the high curve of his butt. The Celtic cross necklace fell at my throat, and he stared into my eyes. "Do you feel what you do to me?" he whispered, brushing the hair off my forehead with gentle fingers.

I nodded. My heartbeat was a roar in my ears.

"I've waited for you for forever, Riley. Do you know that?"

The words were sweet and sincere. I nodded and he smiled softly, before kissing my forehead, then my nose, my lips, my neck...and lower still.

A myriad of emotions rushed through me at the new sensations I was experiencing. Heaven on earth. That's what I felt in every touch. In every kiss.

He was gentle, and I could tell he struggled to stay in control. I could see the need in his eyes, feel it in his touch...and I felt that same desire inside me as my body came to life.

"I want you," I whispered.

"Are you sure?" he said, and at my answering nod, he nudged my thighs apart with his knees and settled between my thighs.

Staring into his blue eyes, I smiled. "Yes, I'm sure."

Kade's cell phone rang on the dock.

A minute later it went off again. Then my phone rang. On it went for several minutes until he sighed under his breath. "Seriously?"

We'd been laying in the sun, cuddled together after making love, and I didn't want the moment to end. Apparently someone else had other plans.

"I better get that, just in case it's Miss Akin." I sat up, reaching for my panties and bra, and sliding them on.

"I'll get it," he said, stepping into his boxer briefs. He kissed me before he slid into the water, and swam in strong strokes to the dock.

I was shocked by the feelings raging inside me, at the utter contentment and happiness I felt. Never could I have imagined feeling this way, this strongly, so soon after meeting Kade. I smiled, already reliving the moments, knowing I'd relive this day for the rest of my life.

He lifted himself up onto the dock effortlessly, his boxer briefs clinging to his high, firm butt. My eyes widened when I recognized the tell-tale signs of my fingernail marks across his shoulders.

Sitting on the dock, he reached into his jeans pocket. He glanced at me in disbelief. "I have five voice messages."

Five. That made me nervous.

"I don't recognize the number." He dialed and listened. "Every single one of them is static."

Static?

Fear rippled along my spine.

Oh my God...Laria.

I immediately eased myself into the water and swam toward the dock. I was more of a side swimmer than a breaststroke or crawl-stroke kind of girl. My parents had sent me to swim lessons when I was little, but for whatever reason, swimming wasn't my forte. I managed, but that was about it.

I was thirty feet away from Kade when I felt her.

I swam faster, and had an urgent, almost overwhelming need to get to safety.

Something brushed my right leg.

I gasped, taking in a mouthful of water. My fingers got caught up in something stringy...like weeds. Or no, was that—hair?

A hand grasped tight to my ankle, and I was abruptly pulled under the water and dragged quickly away from the dock.

I opened my eyes. Laria's face was inches from mine, her long hair floating around her. I tried to get away from her, but her grip on me was too strong. Her hands encircled both my wrists and she tried to pull me deeper under the water.

I heard Kade yell my name, followed by the sound of him diving into the water. Seconds later he was beside me, lifting me up so my head was above the water. "Hold on to my shoulders."

I did as he asked, holding on for dear life as he swam back to the dock.

Kade helped push me up and onto the dock, and then he was beside me, brushing my hair away from my face.

"Riley, are you okay?"

I nodded, unable to believe what had just happened. Laria had tried to kill me, and in front of someone else. In fact, she would have succeeded if Kade hadn't have dove in to save me.

"What happened? You were there one second, and the current must have gotten a hold of you."

I could see him grappling with the questions, given the fact he'd lived here all his life and probably never encountered a current strong enough to drag a swimmer downstream.

"I don't know what happened," I said, uncomfortable when his gaze shifted over my body and lingered on the scars on my ankle—the place where I had cut the most and left the most damage. I made no effort to hide them. "I felt like something got a hold of me and pulled me downstream." It sounded crazy, but it was the truth.

His brows furrowed like he was still trying to understand. That, or he was trying to understand the scars on my body.

He swallowed hard. "I shouldn't have checked my phone. I'm sorry," he said, putting his arm around me and holding me tight. "I should have made sure you were out of the water first."

"I'm fine," I said, settling against him while I scanned the water.

Never in my life could I have imagined that ghosts could be so vengeful. I shuddered. I would never be able to go in the water again without waiting for Laria to pull me down.

I heard a scraping noise come from underneath me. "I should check on Miss Akin," I said, coming to my feet, ready to be as far away from the river as possible.

"Don't you want to dry off first?"

I used my plaid shirt to dry the droplets off my body, and then slid my jeans on and my T-shirt, trying not to look at the cracks between the planks of wood. Why did I have the feeling Laria was still here, still lingering? Just waiting. Had she been here the entire time, even while Kade and I had been making love?

Probably.

Kade dressed quickly and grabbed our fishing poles.

I heard scraping again and made the mistake of looking down between the wooden slats. I swallowed a scream. Laria's dark eyes peered back at me.

"Let's go," I said, and Kade nodded. He took hold of my hand.

I felt him watching me the entire way to the car. The lighthearted feeling of the afternoon had quickly turned, and I couldn't hide the fear I was experiencing. I was already starting to sleep with my bathroom light on. Tonight I doubted I would sleep at all.

"You okay?" Kade asked as he pulled out onto the main highway.

I nodded. "Thanks, I had fun."

"Except for almost drowning." He raked his hands through his dark hair. "I'm so sorry, Riley."

"It's not your fault, and I didn't almost drown. I just drank a little more water than I should have," I said, hoping to lighten the mood.

"I shouldn't have left you out there alone."

His fingers tightened around mine, and I kissed his cheek. I could see the relief in his face as he smiled. A smile that faded as fast as it had come. "Your nose is bleeding."

I lifted my hand to my face and my finger came back with blood.

Not again.

It's like someone turned a faucet on, and I had no choice but to use my plaid shirt as a tissue.

I could feel Kade's growing panic. "You don't think the nosebleed has anything to do from taking on too much water, do you?"

"No, I had a nosebleed the other night, too. It's probably just allergy related."

"You should see a doctor." His thumb brushed along mine, and I smiled, comforted by his concern. "We could drop by the clinic in town."

"Kade, I'm fine."

By the time we pulled into the inn driveway, the nosebleed had stopped.

I invited Kade to stay for a while. Shane was on the computer in Dad's study.

"Hey," I said. "Where's Dad and Miss Akin?"

"Helping clean up at Anne Marie's," Shane said, too into whatever he was reading to look at us. "Dad just called and said they'd be home in an hour or two."

"I'll be upstairs."

"Don't do anything I wouldn't do," he said, finally glancing at us.

One side of his mouth lifted in a smirk before he turned back to the computer.

As Kade and I walked up the stairs, I wondered if I should have checked my room first. Just to see if Laria had been there and made a statement as she was so good at doing.

I turned the doorknob and released the breath I'd been holding.

The room looked just like I'd left it.

Thank God.

Kade walked around the room, taking in everything. "It's just as I thought it would be," he said, stopping at the window. "Too bad you can't see my room from here. We could come up with our own Morse Code using lights."

I smiled.

Turning toward me, his gaze shifted to something over my shoulder.

"Is that Mount Hood?"

My eyes widened. He was talking about the charcoal drawing I'd made when I was fourteen. My mom had entered it in a contest and it had won first place. "Yes. How did you know?"

His brows furrowed. "I don't know. I guess I must have seen it on the Internet or something."

Actually, it wasn't so strange since Ian had commented about the very same picture.

"Could I draw you?"

"Like right now?" he asked, scratching his jaw.

"Yes, right now."

"All right, I'm down for it." He clapped his hands together. "Where do you want me?"

"The chair," I said.

"Clothed or naked?" He maintained a straight face for all of three seconds before flashing a wolfish smile.

"Clothing optional," I said, envisioning Miss A or my dad walking in to find Kade in the altogether. Not a good scenario. "Maybe just lose the shirt."

He reached behind his head, and yanked his shirt off, leaving his hair nice and disheveled—like he'd just woken up.

I pulled paper and charcoal pencils out of the nightstand drawer, and took a seat on the bed. I began with Kade's face, and then made the outline of his body. He had such a beautiful body, all lean muscle and gorgeous olive skin. Memories of the afternoon, of exploring those long lines made me feel all warm inside.

He laughed. "Shouldn't I be the one blushing?"

I couldn't help but smile. "Shh, don't move."

For the next thirty minutes he did as asked, watching me watch him. I remembered when I had drawn Ian, the playful, flirting glances we'd shared. With Kade it was more intense—his stare downright smoldering.

He flexed his muscles a few times and I laughed, telling him to stop it and behave.

"Hey, Tom is having some of us up to his grandparents' cabin Saturday night," Kade said, picking up a ceramic angel that was on my vanity. "Do you want to come?"

I was happy he had asked me. I couldn't wait to spend more time alone with him, and a cabin in the woods, even if it was with our friends, sounded perfect. "Sure, I'd love to."

"It's only about an hour up A-93. I've been there a few times. Nice place, isolated, and there's supposedly a few resident ghosts."

My heart leapt. "Really?"

He nodded. "I haven't seen any, but when Tom was younger he said there was an old lady who stood in his room and watched him sleep."

"Do you believe in ghosts?" I asked, actually anxious to hear his answer.

He tilted his head, eyes narrowing. "Why do you ask?"

I shrugged, and kept my focus on the drawing. "Just curious...I mean you do live in a castle," I said, using the words Madison had thrown at me.

"Do *you* believe in ghosts?"

"No fair, I asked you first."

Taking a deep breath, he released it. "Fair enough...I guess I do then. I've heard noises in the castle that can't be explained, and people who have visited have seen shadows and mists. I mean, if someone dies in a place, then it makes sense that maybe that person's spirit hangs around there."

"When I had dinner at your house, your mom mentioned one of your ancestors being murdered."

"Ian MacKinnon," he said matter-of-factly. "He was poisoned by a female servant who fell in love with him. He wasn't much older than I am now."

My heart was hammering so loud, I was surprised he didn't hear it.

"So did you ever feel his spirit in the castle?"

He shook his head. "I hear noises every once in a while. I think everyone has the sensation of being watched from time to time, and I'm no different. Does that mean my house is full of ghosts? Maybe, but I can't say for sure if it's Ian or not."

What I wouldn't give to be a hundred percent honest with him, and tell him that I had hung out with Ian for weeks. That I felt he was Ian, reincarnated.

"So...is the inn haunted?" he asked.

Actually, I'm the one who is haunted. "Definitely," I said under my breath.

"Really?" he asked, sitting forward. "What have you seen?"

"You don't want to know."

He stared at me for a few seconds, and then the corners of his mouth lifted. "I'll just have to protect you from these ghosts then."

Chapter Twenty-One

Kade had left and I was getting ready for bed when Dad walked into my room. "I wanted to let you know that there is a company party in Edinburgh this weekend."

So he was leaving again. Honestly, I was relieved, especially since I was going to Tom's party with Kade. Maybe I could convince Miss A to let me stay up there overnight...

"And you and Shane are coming with me."

My stomach dropped to my toes. I wanted to hang out with Kade and my friends, not sit through a company party with my dad. "But I already have plans."

"Sorry, but you'll have to break those plans. Everyone in the company is bringing their families, and therefore, I am bringing my family. I've asked Miss Akin along as well," he said, like bringing Miss A would make all the difference in the world.

"Dad, please, I don't want to go."

"I'm sure you like hanging out with your boyfriend, but this is important to me." His voice was stern. "I don't want to hear another word about it. We leave at noon."

Edinburgh was an interesting city. Old, creepy, and yet hauntingly beautiful all at the same time. I felt spirits around me, and although I didn't try to connect, my pulse skittered when I saw the ghost of a young girl, doll in hand, walking up the middle of the Royal Mile. I focused in on her and I got a vision of a mother crying over her, and then covering the girl's face with a pillow.

I flinched. The family had been starving, living in squalor beneath the streets of Edinburgh. A crowded, overrun subterranean apartment that smelled like death.

I pushed away the visions, and followed my family into the hotel. Thank goodness we were staying in the same hotel as the company party. That way we could leave when we wanted, and hopefully my dad wouldn't bitch too much.

Shane and I shared a room, and I watched him closely. He'd gone quiet on me for about an hour, saying very little, but I didn't feel creeped out. No doubt, like me, he was hating his life right now and wishing he was at Tom's party.

Dad dropped by our room at ten minutes to six dressed in a charcoal gray suit. Shane wore a black dress shirt and jeans. He refused to wear slacks, and dad seemed to be content, because he gave us both a once-over and smiled. I wore the sundress I had worn at Milo's birthday party, along with a navy shrug sweater and wedge heels.

The ballroom was full of about two hundred people, and as we ate dinner my dad excused himself, saying he had to use the restroom. He stopped by the table of a lady he'd been eyeing all night. I'd caught a few flirtatious glances between them, but I'd assumed the man sitting beside her was her husband.

That man was now completely turned in his chair, speaking to another woman, their body language familiar.

"This fucking sucks," Shane said under his breath, sliding a little further down into his chair, and pulling his cell phone out of his pocket. Miss A had stayed behind in her room, saying she just wanted to relax and enjoy a movie that was on the History channel. Dad didn't argue, especially since it had been a rough week for her.

I made small talk with the lady to my right, the wife of the Chief Financial Officer of the company. She was sweet, but had horrible breath, and I struggled with trying to keep from inhaling.

Dad walked back toward the table...with the lady he'd been talking to in tow. The man at the table didn't even blink as she left, giving me confirmation that I had been wrong. I elbowed Shane and he sat up, looked at Dad and the woman, and shoved his cell phone back in his jeans pocket.

"Riley, Shane, I'd like you to meet Cheryl Fleming," Dad said, huge grin on his face. I hadn't seen him smile like that since before Mom died. "Cheryl, this is my daughter Riley, and my son Shane."

She had strawberry blonde hair, green eyes, and her forehead had the waxy, kind of startled expression that people who did Botox had. Her tailored suit fit her slim body, and I could tell she was nervous as she reached out and shook Shane's hand and then mine.

My heart sank to my toes. Dad liked her. I could see it in his eyes as he looked at her and smiled reassuringly.

I thought I might puke. My mind started racing, going in a not-so-good direction. Shane had alluded to the fact he thought dad was messing around with someone. Now he glanced at me, his brows lifted as though to say, 'See, I was right.'

My nails bit into my palms.

Shane, looking bored to death, glanced at Dad. "Can I go back to my room now?"

Dad's smile thinned. "The night is young, Shane."

"Dinner is over, though."

Clearing his throat, Dad said, "I'd like for you stay for the CEO's speech."

I felt sick when Dad pulled out a chair beside him and offered it to Cheryl. She held his gaze for a moment, and then with a slight nod, sat down. She immediately started asking questions. Did we like Scotland? How was school? What subjects were we learning? Had we made new friends? Shane answered with one syllable answers, where I tried to be a little more polite. It was tough though... because I knew what this meant. I could tell that my dad wanted us to like her. I could almost feel his desperation.

She said she was divorced, and had an eight-year-old son who went to boarding school in France.

"Lucky him," Shane said under his breath and I smiled inwardly. Personally, I was suspect of anyone who sent their kid to boarding school. My mom had always used boarding school as a threat when we didn't behave. She told us she'd be calling 1-800-boarding school. Little did I realize at the time that the word boarding school had far too many digits to be a phone number. Her threat had worked like a charm, though.

The CEO walked onto the platform and tapped the side of a wine glass with a knife. "Good evening..."

I was actually grateful for the interruption, ready to be out of here and back in my room. I wanted to talk to Kade. How lucky he was that he had both parents, and a great home life.

Shane slid his earbuds in, ignoring Dad's stern look. At least the music wasn't blaring loud enough for the table to hear.

The CEO of Langstrom's Software Services gave one of the most self-inflated speeches I'd ever heard. My mind had wandered and I couldn't help but watch my dad from the corner of my eye. Once I saw him touch Cheryl's hand, and she didn't pull away. He brushed his pinky along her thumb and she glanced up at him with a shy smile.

Bile rose in my throat. So this is why he'd dragged us four thousand miles away from Portland. Another woman. Maybe he was grateful when Mom had been killed in the car wreck. He could play the poor widower to the hilt, and turn around and see his mistress halfway across the world.

I focused on Cheryl, trying to tap into her, but I couldn't focus. My thoughts were all over the place. I was getting more pissed off by the second, and by the time the long-winded speech was over, I stood so fast my chair nearly tipped over. Shane caught it, and righted it before it hit the ground. "I'm heading back to my room. Cheryl, it was nice to meet you." I forced the words past my lips.

"I'll go with you," Shane said. "Nice to meet you, Sandra."

Cheryl opened her mouth to correct him, but Shane was already walking for the double doors. Yep, my brother had returned in force. Thank God.

"Good night," Cheryl replied with a tight smile.

Hotel staff was busy cleaning off tables, and Shane grabbed two glasses of champagne off the back table while the server was preoccupied talking to a guest. He handed me one. I glanced back at the table to see if Dad was watching, but he was talking to Cheryl, and now they were holding hands.

We immediately took a right, toward the stairs and walked the four flights to our room. I tossed back the champagne and left the empty glass on one of the steps.

"Look at you," Shane said, lips quirked. "I'm impressed."

Pulling the room key out of his back pocket, Shane stopped in front of our room and handed me his glass. "Hey, don't drink it."

I was tempted. My heart pounded a mile a minute. I was furious, sad, and disappointed, and all I wanted to do was cry.

The minute the door shut behind us, I turned to Shane. "They're together. I mean, together-together."

"I know." Unbuttoning the dress shirt, he slid it off and put on a T-shirt. "I read Dad's emails to her on his computer."

"How come you didn't say anything?"

He shrugged.

I knew the reason. He didn't want to give me any reason to cut, and he knew Dad dating someone a year after our mom's death was definitely going to upset me. And I was upset. Actually, I was furious. "Do you think they were dating before we moved here?"

"Dad loved Mom, Riley."

"That's not what I asked," I said, sitting on one of the double beds.

"He was probably lonely, and let's face it—he's had business in Edinburgh before. I just choose to believe he wouldn't have screwed around with anyone else while Mom was alive."

"He flew to Edinburgh a few times though." I tried to think back on those times, how Mom acted when he was gone. She never seemed concerned about an affair but then again, some women were completely in the dark about their husband's infidelity.

"Yeah, but I really don't think so. The tone of the emails were more the flirty, new kind of relationship emails. You know what I mean?"

I suppose I did. It still didn't help though. I felt like it was way too early for him to move on.

"Hey, look at the bright side." He flashed a grin. "This means he'll be gone even more now."

"I can't believe you just said that."

"I'm not trying to be an insensitive dick, but what can we do, Ri? He's lonely, and now he's found someone. He can spend his weeks and weekends in Edinburgh, and Miss A can keep an eye on us. She's a lot easier to deal with than Dad."

So true. Thank God for Miss A. She was our salvation. "Do you think he brought Miss A along as a buffer?"

"Definitely." He chewed his thumbnail. "He probably figured this was the easiest way to let us know about her. Whatever the case—he's moving on. We have to accept it."

The problem was...I didn't want to accept it.

I went into the bathroom, washed my face, and changed into my pajamas. Shane was slumped against the headboard, feet crossed at the ankles, scrolling through the channels. The hotel only had basic cable. Aside from an old movie that wasn't good the first time we'd watched it, we were stuck with watching reality television, Scottish style.

"This fucking sucks," Shane said around ten. "We're missing one hell of a party."

I nodded in agreement, and sent yet another text message to Megan. No one was responding—not Kade, not Cait, not Cassandra or Megan.

"You have any luck getting your friends?" I asked Shane.

He shook his head. "Milo forewarned me there's little to no mobile reception at the cabin, so I'm not surprised."

We spent the next hour in silence. I had hoped my phone would ring and I'd get an update from Megan, or at least hear from Kade... but nothing.

Shane went to the bathroom and turned on the fan. I heard the click of his lighter. "I thought you quit that," I said, figuring he couldn't hear me over the fan when he didn't respond.

"Only in case of emergencies...and this is an emergency." He poked his head out, the joint pinched between his fingers. "You want a drag?"

"No thanks."

Within thirty minutes he was asleep and I was staring at the ceiling. I picked up my cell phone, dialed Kade's number and then hit *End.* It was after midnight. I didn't want to act desperate, even though I was.

Glancing at Shane one last time, I set my phone aside and slid under the covers.

Chapter Twenty-Two

I was at Tom's party, a cottage with three bedrooms, a great room, kitchen and a loft. I had a drink in my hand and as I walked through the crowd, people nodded at me. Kade stood with his friends, leaning against the kitchen counter, a cup full of beer in hand. Seeing me, he nodded and continued talking with his friends. I'd expected a more enthusiastic reaction, and rather than go up to him, I stayed on the periphery and waited for him to come to me.

I lingered nearby, drinking, and talking with friends. When he walked past me, I grabbed his hand and led him into the nearest bedroom.

"What are you doing?" he asked, perplexed and irritated as he pulled his hand away.

"Don't you want me?" I asked, but it wasn't my voice. I did the strangest thing then—I put my hand to his forehead, and then flaring my fingers, slid them down over his face.

He blinked a few times and stared at me for about ten seconds before his lips curved into a boyish smile, white teeth flashing. "What are you doing here?"

Before I could answer, he leaned in and kissed me like he hadn't seen me in weeks.

Liquid fire rushed through my veins, and I savored the way his hands ran over my body. Desperate to get closer, my fingers threaded through his dark hair, and I clung to his shoulders.

Knocking sounded at the door and Kade cursed under his breath. "Go away."

"Come on, MacKinnon. Not in my parents' room. Go upstairs to the loft, will ya?"

He took my hand and opened the door. Tom stood there, brow lifted high as his gaze shifted between us. One side of his mouth curved in a strange, kind of knowing smile. He shook his head a second later and wandered back into the kitchen.

I pulled Kade's head down to mine and we kissed. I could hear his friends whispering, and Johan laughed. Maybe too much PDA for them?

Kade caught my earlobe with his teeth. Goosebumps rose along my arms and I smiled. As we walked into the great room, I saw Richie, Shane's friend, who sat on one of the two couches playing video games with Tom's brother. He glanced at us, and did a quick double-take, his gaze focused on our linked hands. Frowning, he turned back to his game, looking confused.

We walked up the stairs to the loft, hand in hand.

I caught my reflection in an oval mirror hanging on the wall. My eyes looked strange, different. He grabbed me, kissing me, pulling me close.

My arms encircled his neck, and when I glanced in the mirror again, this time I saw someone else's reflection.

I woke from the dream with a sickening feeling. The dream had seemed so real. What if Kade really had been with Dana?

No, I was just getting myself riled up. All my fears about not being able to go to the party had manifested into a nightmare, that's all. I was just freaking myself out unnecessarily.

I took a shower and got dressed. Shane was still sleeping, so instead of turning on the television, I sat in a chair by the window and texted Megan, asking her about the party.

Within five minutes she texted back saying she and Cassandra had left the party at eleven thirty, but it had been fun and she was bummed I had missed it.

I was relieved. If something had happened, Megan would tell me. I knew that. We were good enough friends to have each other's backs, and I knew Cassandra couldn't keep anything to herself. She would have definitely texted me by now. I'd feel even better once I talked to Kade.

Dad came knocking on our door at ten o'clock and said we were having brunch. I just wanted to get home, but it's not like I had a choice. I felt a strange sense of urgency that only intensified when I saw Cheryl sitting at a table in the dining room. Seeing us, she waved and we followed Dad and Miss Akin over.

Cheryl wore jeans and a sweater and her slightly longer than shoulder-length hair was worn down. She was prettier without so much makeup, I thought, but she would never be as pretty as my mom. No amount of makeup would change that.

Miss Akin kept the conversation flowing during brunch, mostly about the beauty of Edinburgh. I couldn't eat a bite. After last night's dream and the knowledge that Dad had a girlfriend, I had no appetite. I couldn't say the same about Shane though, who downed his breakfast and then mine on top of it.

When Dad checked out at the hotel desk and said goodbye to

Cheryl, Miss Akin put a hand around my shoulder and squeezed. "We'll be home soon, my dear."

My irritation must have been obvious. I managed a halfhearted, "Nice to meet you," to Cheryl when we parted ways in the parking garage.

None of us said a word as we walked to the car and settled in for the ride home.

Dad slipped into the car and he had lipstick on his mouth. Pink lipstick. The same shade as Cheryl's.

He even started whistling.

My gut clenched.

As he pulled out onto the main highway, I saw him watch me and Shane in the rearview mirror, almost like he was waiting for us to say something about his girlfriend. What did he expect us to say? "Hey, thanks for completely blindsiding us."

I avoided his gaze, and instead stared out the window. Shane sat beside me, listening to his iPod. We were an hour into our ride when his phone signaled he had a text. He hit a button, read the text, and then he lifted the screen closer to his face. He sat up straighter, glanced at me from the corner of his eye, and then started texting.

Probably a porno picture from Richie, who was rumored to send raunchy pics and videos to his friends' phones and emails.

I held my phone in my hand, cranked my music and stared out at the passing landscape for the next hour.

When Dad pulled into the inn driveway, I opened the door even before he stopped the car. I already had my backpack in hand, and wished I'd thought to bring my key along so I didn't have to wait for Dad to unlock the front door. He watched me closely but I refused to make eye contact. I did glance at Shane. His earbuds hung around his neck, and he had pocketed his phone.

Once the door was open, I walked past everyone and ran up the stairs. In my room, I pulled open the drapes and looked out at the castle. My heart pounded hard against my chest. Over and over again the scene from the dream replayed itself in my mind.

Something was very wrong. I felt it in my bones.

I glanced at my phone. No messages, no missed calls. It was nearly three o'clock in the afternoon. Why the hell hadn't Kade called by now?

I set the phone on my nightstand. I needed to focus on something else.

I thumbed through Laria's journal, and couldn't help but wonder why she had suddenly gone quiet. Too quiet.

A knock sounded at my door. I so didn't want to talk to my dad about Cheryl. "Come in."

Shane opened the door and shut it behind him. "Hey."

"Hey, what's up?" I asked, sitting down on my bed.

"I have to tell you something," he said hesitantly.

Every nerve in my body tensed. "Okay."

"Richie was at Tom's party last night...and he said that Kade was with Dana."

Tears burned my eyes, and I tried to blink them back but failed. In the dream I had seen Dana's reflection in the mirror. This just confirmed that the dream had been real.

"I'm sorry, Ri," Shane said giving me a hug. "I know you really like him."

Actually, I loved him.

I put Shane at arm's length. "Were they like together-together?"

He winced. "I don't know for sure, but it doesn't look good."

"Look? What do you mean?"

He handed me his cell phone and hit the video play button.

There in full color was Kade making out with Dana. Every nerve in my body tensed. He had her up against the wall in the hallway, one hand in her hair, the other on her ass. I could hear Tom in the background laughing under his breath. No doubt he'd taken the video. "Richie said they went up to the loft right after that was filmed, and didn't come down for an hour."

My imagination, or memory of the vision, had to fill in the gaps of what happened in that hour.

"How did you get the video?"

"Richie. He texted me first thing this morning, asking if you and Kade had broke up. I didn't want to say anything when we were in the car. I didn't want Dad and Miss A to hear."

I couldn't hold the flood of tears back any longer. I was devastated.

"I'm sorry, Ri." Shane gave me another hug, his arms tight around me. "He'll be sorry. I guarantee it."

Kade stopped by a little after five o'clock, and I could hear him talking to Shane at the front door.

I almost went downstairs when I heard my dad intervene. A few seconds later the front door closed and I heard a car pull out of the driveway. I didn't want to talk to my dad about Kade or what had happened. In a way I blamed him for taking me to Edinburgh when I could have been with my boyfriend instead. I was sure Miss A would catch on soon enough, and show up at my bedroom door with milk and cookies.

Milk and cookies were the last thing I needed.

My phone rang. It was Kade's number. I immediately turned the phone off.

I needed a lobotomy, or anything that would get the image of Kade and Dana all over each other out of my mind. Unfortunately every second of the fifty-four second footage was burned into my memory. There was nothing he could do or say to deny it—it was there for all to see in living color.

Disappointment and anger ate at my insides. I hated the dark feelings waging war inside of me. I was furious, hurt, humiliated, and I wished more than anything I would have been home this weekend.

I shook my head, unable to believe Kade had hurt me so badly. Ian would have never betrayed me. No way, not like this. I took out the drawings of Ian and Kade, my gaze skipping from one to the other. I clenched the drawing of Kade in my fist and tossed it across the room.

I closed my eyes, took a deep breath in and tried to focus on something positive, but there was nothing positive in my life...aside from my friends. But not one of them could make me feel better.

With a sigh, I opened my eyes and saw the matchbox. Laying at the end of the bed. My heart missed a beat. Where had it come from? It hadn't been there seconds ago.

Do it.

I snatched up the box, opened it. My hand trembled seeing the single, sparkling new razor blade. I craved the release it would give me—knew that the pent-up rage toward Kade, the hatred toward Dana, and the frustration I felt with my father would disappear, if only for a minute.

I walked into the bathroom, and shut the door behind me. Without a second thought, I brought the razor blade to my arm and dragged it across my flesh.

The blood beaded on my skin, and I waited for the familiar release to come.

Instead, as the seconds ticked into minutes, I felt an overwhelming sense of anger and disappointment at myself. Tears burned my eyes. What the hell had I done? I had promised myself I would never cut again.

Cruel laughter filled my ears. A wave of nausea washed over me as I watched the trail of blood drip from my arm, onto the floor.

I was so tired. Tired of life. Tired of everything and everyone.

"Riley."

I heard my name being called, sounding like from a distance.

I tried to open my eyes, but my lids were so heavy.

"Riley, wake up."

Slowly, I opened my eyes to find my brother standing over me, a look of shock on his face. "No, no, no," he was saying over and over again.

I blinked, and when I focused on him, he was ravaging through the medicine cabinet. "What the hell are you thinking?" I could hear the anger in his voice.

I understood why he was pissed. I was angry with myself.

I glanced at the cut, surprised the blood had dried so quickly…or had I passed out?

"I shouldn't have said anything about Kade. God damn it," he said under his breath.

He was on his haunches beside me, pouring hydrogen peroxide over the wound.

It stung like hell, but I welcomed the pain.

"You told me you wouldn't cut," he said through clenched teeth.

"I'm sorry, Shane."

Grabbing a wad of cotton balls, he pressed several to the cut.

"I don't know...you might need stitches."

"I'll be fine."

An awkward silence followed, and I watched him work methodically, placing butterfly bandages over the cut. When he was finished, he stood and held his hand out to me. "Megan and Cassandra are downstairs."

Honestly, I didn't want to see anyone. I just wanted to lay in bed, and curl into the fetal position. "Tell them I'll see them tomorrow."

He nodded, and started for the door, but stopped short. "Things will get better, Riley. You'll see. Don't let this beat you."

Easier said than done. What would he say if I told him the truth about everything? About Laria, and how she had her hooks into both of us.

Chapter Twenty-Three

The following morning it took everything within me to get out of bed. Of course, I knew Kade and Dana would be the talk of school. No doubt the video had gone viral and everyone knew that my boyfriend was a douchebag.

"Keep your chin up," Shane said as we walked through the double doors. He'd kept a vigil on me through the night, and only left my side to get cleaned up this morning. I had tried to make an effort this morning to look good, and maybe remind Kade of what a mistake he had made, but my hair wouldn't cooperate, so I'd thrown it into a high ponytail. I was pale, and I had circles under my eyes.

I pulled the sweater tighter around me, and took a deep, steadying breath. "Thanks, I'll be fine."

"Good girl," he said, nodding to one of his friends, who flashed a sympathetic smile my way.

And it begins... I thought.

Megan and Cassandra rounded the corner, and seeing me, they rushed my way, concern on both their faces. I was glad they had stopped by last night, and in hindsight I wished I would have talked to them rather than crying myself to sleep.

"See you later," Shane said, leaving me in the company of my buddies.

"Sorry, Ri. Honestly," Megan said, giving me a hug.

Cassandra squeezed my hand in a rare show of affection. "We left the cabin before the porno action went down."

"Jesus, Cass—would it kill you to be a little sympathetic?" Megan said, shaking her head. "You know we would have called you had we seen or heard anything, Riley. And I came over last night right after Milo told me."

"You're good friends," I said, meaning it. I was grateful to have them both.

I straightened when I saw Dana standing by her locker, a triumphant smile on her face as she watched me walk by.

I wanted to jump her and rip her eyes out. Instead, I kept my spine straight, shoulders back, and told myself I was better than she was. I refused to play the victim.

"Whore." Cassandra mouthed the word, flashing Dana the one-finger salute as we walked by.

Just seeing Dana reminded me of the video.

God, I wanted to move back to Portland. Being invisible was better than being made a fool of. I felt stupid, used, and discarded... and I wished more than anything I hadn't given my V-card to Kade MacKinnon.

Biggest.

Mistake.

Of.

My.

Life.

This weekend had been the worst on record. My new boyfriend

had cheated on me, and my dad was seeing a woman and replacing my mom.

Could my life suck more?

I went to my locker, and as I approached I saw a picture taped to the outside.

As I came closer, my heart took a nosedive. A picture of a blonde cutting herself.

"What's that?" Megan asked.

I ripped the picture off the locker door and crushed it in my fist. What a vindictive bitch. First she'd screwed around with my boyfriend and now she was announcing to the school that I cut.

Megan and Cassandra looked at each other, and I could tell by their expressions that they had seen the picture. I could feel my world shattering into pieces...again.

"Here comes Cait," Cassandra said a second later.

Cait was alone, her skirts bouncing with each step. She walked with purpose, straight for me, and I knew what was coming even before she opened her mouth. "Riley, my brother needs to talk to you."

"I have nothing to say to him."

She was disappointed. "Riley, I know you're mad...but please hear him out."

"Leave her alone, Cait. Christ, you weren't even there," Cassandra said, sounding irritated. "Hasn't she been through enough?"

Turning to Cait, she opened her mouth, then snapped it shut just as quickly. "You're right—I wasn't there, but I do believe my brother when he says he thought Dana was Riley."

Cassandra snorted. "Really? You're buying that?"

"I've seen the video," I said, brushing a hand through my hair. "I don't need any more evidence to know it happened."

"Just please let him explain."

"What would you do, Cait? What would you do if you were in my shoes?"

"I know it looks bad...but he honestly said he thought it was you."

In the dream I remembered his reaction when I'd first seen him. Kind of like he was blowing me off. And when I'd touched his face, he'd blinked a few times and reacted completely different. Hadn't he also asked, 'What are you doing here?' like he hadn't expected me to be there?

I shook my head. What was I thinking? He could have been saying that to Dana, who had a tendency to always show up where she wasn't invited.

"Cait, I appreciate you trying to make things better, but honestly, right now I don't care if I ever see him again."

Cait opened her mouth, but Megan shook her head. "Let it go, Cait. I know he's your brother and all, but he's a bloody wanker."

Johan walked by, and his expression was difficult to read. I remembered him in the dream, the way he'd laughed. Since he figured I'd blown him off this summer, he was probably happy to see me get hurt by Kade.

"I'll see you guys later," I said, grabbing my textbook and slamming the locker.

Unfortunately, Dana beat me to first period. She sat in the front row, hands folded on the desk, back arched, cleavage on display for all to see.

"Cutter," she said as I walked by.

I could feel the blood drain from my face.

I glanced at her friend, the virgin. She wasn't making eye contact.

I tried to block out the image of Kade and Dana all over each other while laughing their asses off about him taking my virginity. The *cutter's* virginity.

Why should I be so surprised? Secrets never did stay buried for very long. I knew that.

Aaron sat down, and he turned to me, caramel-colored eyes intense. He reached out, touched my hand. "Don't listen to her, Riley. She's trash."

I forced a smile I didn't feel, my gaze shifting to his hand. I saw the tiny scars on the inside of his wrist.

My gaze skipped to his and he abruptly turned back around.

Dana watched our exchange and shook her head, like she thought I was pathetic.

I would show them all that I could survive this. I was stronger than they would ever guess, and the last thing I would do is let them see me crumble.

That strength started to waver as the afternoon wore on. I stayed in the library during lunch, unable to handle seeing Kade. People could call me weak or whatever. I had turned my phone off after seeing the pictures, and with the way I was feeling, I could crush the phone into a thousand pieces.

I had hoped to talk to Peter, but all day my efforts to connect had been unsuccessful. Damn, I could use his help. I needed answers and it was time to pick his brain.

Through the small rectangular window in the library door, I saw Kade approach. I scrambled up from my spot. There was only one other person in the library, a student who worked the front desk. I put a finger to my lips. She nodded as I walked behind a shelf of books.

I could hear Kade asking about me. I breathed a sigh of relief when I heard the library aide reply, "Sorry, haven't seen her."

I kept my head down the rest of the day, ignoring everyone and everything. I heard the whispers about Kade and Dana, though.

After school, I waited for Megan, who had to stay after to speak to a teacher about extra credit for an assignment she'd failed. By the time we walked into the parking lot, I was relieved to see the busses had left and the parking lot had emptied out, except for the athletes and kids in detention. Milo's van was among those cars.

"Riley!"

It was Kade, yelling for me from near the field.

"Bloody hell," Megan said, sliding her hand around my arm and picking up her pace.

From the corner of my eye, I saw him walking toward me in long strides.

"Riley, please...I need to talk to you." I could hear the desperation in his voice.

I nearly broke into a run, but stopped myself short. Why should I run? I hadn't done anything wrong. I stopped, closed my eyes, and took a deep breath. "I'll be right there."

"I'll be at the car," Megan said reluctantly.

I nodded. Before I could change my mind, I turned.

He looked like he hadn't slept in days. Wearing navy track pants and a white wife-beater that formed to his chiseled body, I forced myself to meet his gaze. Deep, dark purple half-circles bracketed his beautiful blue eyes.

I loved him.

I hated him.

I wanted to disappear.

His gaze shifted over me, like he hadn't seen me for years. "I know it sounds crazy, but I swear to God I thought it was you, Riley. Half the night is a blur. I can't remember much of anything, but I do remember seeing you."

My heart was beating so loud; it was a roar in my ears. "You might want to look at the video circulating around school. Maybe that will refresh your memory."

He flinched like I'd slapped him. "You were there," he said, almost to himself. "It was you."

My mind was jumbled with images of the video, but also of the dream I'd had. I'd seen myself in the mirror's reflection...but then I had turned into Dana in the blink of an eye.

He reached out, grabbed my hand, his fingers holding me tight. "I would never hurt you. You know that—" The words died on his lips.

"I can't do this." I pulled my hand away.

Running a hand down his face, he stared at me, his gaze imploring me to understand. He was actually trembling.

It was on the tip of my tongue to ask him how Dana knew about my cutting, but I couldn't ask. Maybe I didn't want to hear the answer. I'm sure he would say he didn't remember that part of the night either.

"I have to go," I said, turning on my heel and heading for Megan's car.

"Please." He reached out, grabbed my arm. "I wish I wouldn't have gone to that party. Riley, I want you. I don't want anyone else. I swear to God."

I could see the desperation in his eyes. He wanted—no—he *needed* me to understand.

"Drop her fuckin' hand, MacKinnon."

It was Shane. Dressed for practice, he stepped between us and

Kade had no choice but to drop my arm.

"I'm just trying to explain the other night," Kade said, sounding defeated.

"Dude, she doesn't want to hear your excuses."

A nerve in Kade's jaw twitched.

"MacKinnon, Williams, get over here!" Coach Everson stood by the fence, hands on hips, watching our every move. I was sure he wasn't about to let his star player get into a fight. The star player who would have a long line of girls waiting to take my place.

Shane glanced back at Kade. He took a step toward him and lowered his voice. "You're an asshole, and if you ever come near my sister again, I'll knock your fuckin' head off your shoulders."

Kade glanced from Shane to me. "Please Riley. We need to talk."

"Dude, she has nothing to say to you!" Shane turned toward me. "Ri, go home. I'll see you at dinner."

I nodded and walked toward Megan. I didn't even look at Kade. I couldn't. I was over it. I was over hurting.

Chapter Twenty-Four

I'm sorry.

It was the tenth text of the day from Kade. I promptly hit *Delete* and went back to attempting to read the chapter for history. I don't know why I bothered trying to focus on homework; it was no use. I couldn't get Kade out of my mind or the conversation we'd had.

What if Laria had done something to make Kade believe I was there? She had masqueraded as my mom before, and it had taken some heavy convincing on Ian's part before I realized I'd been duped and it had been Laria masquerading as my mom.

I replayed the dream from the other night in my mind, and the conversation with Kade where he'd insisted it was me at the party. Once again I thought of what he'd said in the dream, the surprise on his face when he'd seen me, where he'd had no interest in me seconds before.

The surprise on his face would have been the same surprise he would have had if I'd shown up at the party unannounced.

Everything pointed toward Laria's involvement.

"Riley, dinner is ready," Miss Akin called from the kitchen.

I dreaded facing Shane, and even more, my dad. I was still angry with him about Edinburgh. He had a girlfriend. I knew that, and although Cheryl seemed like a nice lady, she wasn't my mom and I felt a sense of betrayal that I couldn't let go of. He could have told us about her before introducing her to us like she was just a co-worker.

Granted, I didn't want my dad to be alone for the rest of his life...but the loss of my mom was still too new. Christ, couldn't he at least wait until we were graduated and out of the house before he moved on? I could see it now—a marriage ensuing, Cheryl moving her son in—well, at least on holidays. And hey—why wouldn't she send us off to boarding school if she shipped her own kid off to a different country?

I shook away the disturbing thought. God, I seriously hated my life.

Setting the book aside, I headed down the stairs. Wearing flannel pajama pants and a navy long john shirt, I walked down the hallway, and stopped short at the top of the stairs.

Cold air surrounded me, and I closed my eyes for a second and took a few steadying breaths. I hoped it was Peter. I missed the little shit; his sense of humor, and his companionship would be a welcome relief right about now. I wondered where he had been, or if it had just been me being lost in my own world, that I had closed off my abilities. In the books I'd read it talked about being blocked, especially during times of stress.

I was definitely stressed.

The front door opened and closed. Shane glanced up at me. "Hey, you okay?" he asked, kicking off his shoes.

"I'm fine," I said when I was shoved hard from behind.

Shane's eyes widened, and I heard him yell my name a second

before the whole world went black.

I heard a buzzing noise overhead, like the sound of halogen lights.

"I just don't understand," I heard my dad say. "Shane, tell me again what happened?"

A sharp pain shot through my skull. The smell of antiseptic was strong, and my entire body was sore.

"She was pushed," Shane said. "One second she was standing at the top of the stairs, the next she was falling."

"That's ridiculous." Dad sounded agitated.

"Whatever," Shane said, his frustration obvious. "You weren't there. I was."

Leave it to Dad to think we'd brainstormed the whole episode. Seriously, I had other ways to get his attention rather than pitching myself down a flight of stairs.

"Miss Akin mentioned that Riley has been having a tough couple of days," a woman with an American accent said. "What can you tell me about that, Mr. Williams?"

I kept my eyes closed on purpose, waiting for the answer to that question.

"Well...um, she seems to be fine." I didn't have to open my eyes to know Dad was staring at Shane, hoping he'd cough up information.

I held my breath and waited for Shane to spill.

He said nothing, no doubt enjoying Dad's discomfort at being put on the spot. And as the silent seconds ticked by, it became blatantly obvious that he knew squat about what was going on in his own kids' lives.

"Isn't that right, Shane?"

Shane grunted.

When silence fell over the group, I slowly opened my eyes. I was in a small room with white and green tile everywhere and a picture of a waterfall on the ceiling directly over the bed. Three faces looked down at me, each looking relieved in their own way. Shane gave me a glance, like he knew I'd been listening for a while. The doctor's brows were furrowed in a straight line. Dad was the first to speak. "How are you, sweetheart?"

"Okay," I replied.

The doctor, a tall lady with graying hair and a young-looking face pushed her glasses up her nose. "What happened, exactly, Miss Williams?"

"I was pushed down the stairs."

Dad frowned. "Honey, there was no one in the house but you, your brother and Miss Akin, and neither of them were near you when the accident occurred."

Shane crossed his arms over his chest and mouthed the word 'asshole.' I smiled inwardly. Yep, my brother was back, thank God. Problem was, Laria was making herself known in other ways.

Dad put a hand on my forehead. "I'm sure there's a completely logical explanation."

A nursing assistant walked in. "The x-rays are up."

The doctor nodded and walked over to the laptop. A minute later she pulled up my scan. "The x-ray shows a mild sign of concussion. She should probably stay home from school for a few days."

Dad nodded obediently, and scratched his chin. "Of course."

"If you two will step out of the room while I examine her..."

My dad shot to his feet. "Come on, Shane."

"We'll be out in the waiting room," Dad said, and I nodded.

The doctor took a seat on a stool next to the bed. "Hello, Riley. My name is Dr. Ronson."

"Hello."

"You took a nasty fall. Walk me through it, step by step."

I had heard Shane explain what had happened to her just seconds before, but apparently she wanted to hear it from me. "I was standing at the top of the stairs when I must have lost my footing."

She nodded, and wrote something down in the chart. "You'll have more bruising tomorrow."

She glanced up. "I noticed some scarring on your legs, sides and arms."

I felt my cheeks turn hot. "They're just scratches."

"They are pretty deep wounds to be scratches, Riley. In fact, one is bandaged."

I shifted on the gurney, wishing I could get away from her intense stare. I just wanted to head home, go to bed, and forget about the past few days.

"I am good friends with a counselor who might be able to help you."

"I don't need any help."

She pressed her lips together and wrote in the chart. "I need to say something to your father about the cuts."

"Please don't. He has enough to worry about."

"You're a minor." She put a hand on my shoulder and smiled reassuringly. "There are other ways to deal with grief, Riley."

"Like medication?" I said, unable to keep the sarcasm from my voice. "I've tried that. I'd rather not spend my life sleep-walking."

"There are support groups which have proved beneficial to many teens suffering from grief."

I had no interest sitting in a circle with people as messed up as I was, sharing all the things that made our lives so depressing.

She spent the next fifteen minutes putting me through a series of tests. When she was finished, she grabbed the folder and brought it to her chest. "You're a very lucky girl, Riley. I'm surprised you don't have more symptoms. I want to see you back here next Monday."

"Okay."

"You'll be okay. Time helps. I lost my mother when I was thirteen."

I heard the word cancer and saw blackened lungs in my mind's eye. "Cancer?"

The doctor nodded. "Yes, of the lungs. How did you know?"

"I guessed," I blurted, glad I wasn't as blocked as I'd feared.

"She was gone within three weeks of diagnosis, which is the main reason I became a doctor." She shook her head, as though shaking away the memory. "Anyway, you will be better with time. I promise."

The car ride home was sobering. My dad kept glancing over at me, his hands gripped tightly around the steering wheel. Shane stared out the window, his finger tapping in time to the music blaring from his iPod.

When we pulled into the driveway, Miss Akin was waiting at the door for us. Seeing her, I felt the urge to throw myself into her arms and cry my eyes out. Sometimes I think she was the only person on earth who understood me. The only person, aside from Shane, who really cared about me.

"You'll be fine, my dear," she said, smoothing a hand over the back of my head. "Let's get you to bed. You must be exhausted."

Ten minutes later I was in bed, a warm blanket wrapped around my legs and Miss Akin spoon-feeding me chicken noodle soup. I wasn't even hungry, but she insisted. "The doctor prescribed some pills for pain but you must have something in your stomach."

My head hurt like hell, but the last thing I wanted to do was take a painkiller and get buzzed out of my mind. No need to make Laria's crusade to kill me any easier. Miss A popped open the pill container, and handed me an oval white pill. "Here you go." She handed me a glass of water, watched as I drank it, and then tucked me in.

I woke up once to find Shane sleeping on the floor beside my bed.

I smiled and rolled over. By the time morning came, he was gone and I could smell the familiar scent of sausage and eggs permeating from downstairs.

A few soft taps sounded at my door. "Come in, Miss A."

"It's Dad." He stepped into my room. Wearing his usual slacks and a white button-down shirt over a white T-shirt.

"How do you feel?"

"My head hurts a little, but I think I can go to school tomorrow."

I hated that I couldn't go today, knowing what everyone would think—that I had bailed because I was mortified by Kade and Dana.

"I barely slept last night," he said, taking a seat in the chair. His tense body language alone spoke volumes.

I sat up against the headboard, knowing exactly where the conversation was headed.

"There's no easy way for me to broach this subject, Riley...so I'll just dive right in. Dr. Ronson asked me about the marks on your body. She said that it looked like you had cut yourself."

I swallowed hard and I dropped my gaze to the floor between us. I had dreaded this conversation. As much as I'd like to deny it, I wouldn't.

"I searched the Internet last night reading about your disorder."

My disorder?

"There are inpatient programs available—places where you stay for six months or so…and are treated."

So he was going to ship me off now? Panic seized me. "I don't need a program." If it weren't for Laria constantly planting the razor blades in my room, I wouldn't have gone looking for them.

His brows lifted. "You have a fresh cut on your elbow, Riley, as well as scratches on your back and arms."

He leaned his elbows on his knees. "Make me understand this, Riley. What on earth would cause you to cut yourself?"

There were so many things, none of which he would ever understand, so I didn't even want to waste my breath.

"Dr. Ronson suggested you talk to a psychiatrist."

My so-called psychiatric treatment back in Portland had nearly put me into a walking coma. I'd spent the better part of my day in bed, completely numb. "I don't need a psychiatrist, Dad."

"You are cutting yourself on purpose." The way he looked at me…as though I were damaged goods, made me sick. "You need a psychiatrist, Ri."

"I miss Mom," I blurted. This was one of those times I needed to feel her arms around me, to have her pull me tight and reassure me that everything would be okay.

"I miss her, too, Riley…but I don't hurt myself, for God's sake."

No, he just replaced her with another woman.

"I thought you liked it here. You have good friends. Miss Akin says you keep busy." He shook his head. "I don't get it, Riley."

"I don't expect you to *get it*, Dad. You never lost your mom."

"No, but I lost my wife."

"I spent more time with her than you ever did." I could barely believe I'd said the words.

Apparently Dad thought the same thing because his eyes narrowed. "What did you say?"

"You were never home. You live for your work. You always have and you always will."

He shook his head. I had surprised him, and not in a good way. "I find comfort in work; there's nothing wrong with that."

"What about finding comfort in your family? You have two kids who would give anything for you to care. We crave your attention."

He pulled a tissue from his pocket and blew his nose. "I'm doing the best I can."

"Really?" I asked, my heart slamming against my chest wall. "Because from where I'm sitting, it looks like you're running away from your life and what family you do have left. The only time you talk to me or Shane is when you want to complain about something we've done."

"That's not fair."

Tears slipped from my eyes, and I didn't bother to brush them away. "It's the truth."

"I'll be calling Dr. Ronson today," he said, standing, signaling the conversation was over. As usual, he would rather run than face confrontation.

"Don't bother," I said, getting out of bed and walking toward my closet.

"Where do you think you're going?"

I turned to him. "To school." I wasn't going to have people talking more shit about me.

He walked toward the door. "Get to school, Shane."

"Hasn't she been through enough without you all over her ass?"

Shane asked, hands on hips.

I could tell by his expression alone Dad was ready to lose it. He looked at Shane. "Don't tell me what to do. I'm the adult here."

Shane's eyes narrowed. "You could have fooled me."

My dad lifted his hand, like he was going to strike him and Shane's brow lifted. "Wow, really?"

Dad's mouth opened, like he couldn't quite believe what he'd just about done.

Tears burned my eyes. I didn't want to go back to this dark place...but I was there, and I could almost hear Laria's laughter vibrating in my ears. My life was unraveling and I could do nothing to stop it.

"Shane, I didn't. I wouldn't—" He shook his head, and reached out to Shane.

Shane stepped away and he glanced at me. "Riley, you need to stay home today. You can't go to school. I won't allow it."

"Your brother is right," Dad said, remembering that he was the parent. "I won't press the counselor, but if you feel like you need anything or want to talk to anyone, I want you to know that help is available."

I nodded and watched as they walked out of the room. A minute later the front door opened and closed.

Miss Akin brought me breakfast and another pain pill. I ate a few bites of sausage and eggs, and swallowed a pill. I lay down, exhausted but grateful to just be able to shut off the real world and surrender to my dreams.

Those dreams were scattered; due to the opiates, I was sure. I woke up once to use the bathroom, and I swore someone had been standing near my bathroom door. With my heart in my throat, I felt a momentary panic that quickly faded when I turned on the light to find no one there.

When I fell back to sleep I had a dream about Ian, and we sat on the hillside looking out over Braemar. His head was in my lap as my fingers wove through his dark, long hair. I told him how much I missed him and that I wanted him back...and he had told me he was with me. That our souls were back together, as one.

I asked him to explain what he meant; he pulled my head down to his and he kissed me. When I opened my eyes it wasn't Ian but Kade laying there, looking up at me. In the dream I didn't miss a beat. "You're the same," I said to him, and he nodded and smiled, his familiar eyes full of love. He took one of my hands in his, placed it on his chest. "Aye, we're the same soul, Riley...and we're together again."

The same soul...which meant the same person.

I opened my eyes, wishing immediately that I would go back to that dream. Every muscle in my body ached...but not as much as my heart ached.

Chapter Twenty-Five

Megan and Cassandra showed up right after school. We sat in my room, Cassandra painting her toenails with black fingernail polish, and Megan with hot pink. I had considered using black polish like Cassandra, something that matched my mood, but instead decided on a neutral brown. Cassandra immediately pushed my hands away. "Let me do that," she said, and began painting my toes.

Miss Akin had been babying me all day, and it was nice to get added attention from my friends. It felt great to be cared for.

"I can't believe you fell down the stairs." Megan shuddered. "How scary."

"I told you I was a klutz."

Her lips quirked. "You weren't kidding, huh?"

"Dana said you threw yourself down the steps for sympathy," Cassandra said, blowing a bubble with her gum.

Megan shook her head. "What the hell is the matter with you, Cass?"

Cassandra frowned. "What?"

"It's okay." I was tired of everyone tiptoeing around me about Kade.

Megan stuck her hand out and looked at her nails, then at me. "Kade actually cornered me today in study hall and asked about you."

I shifted on the bed.

"He swore to me he doesn't remember anything about Dana. I almost want to believe him."

Cassandra snorted. "Wouldn't we all like to say we didn't remember a bloody thing after a regretful hook up? If the tables were turned and you would have shagged another guy, he would never forgive you."

"That's not true." Megan breathed on her nails. "I mean, Kade is different...and you don't know for sure if he shagged her or not."

"Can we drop it," I said, not wanting or needing the visual that came with the accusation.

"Done," Cassandra replied. "Hey, are you going to the game on Friday? Me, Megan and Cait are going. It's against our arch nemesis."

By Friday I would definitely want to be leaving this room and the inn. "Sure. Hopefully Shane will play."

Megan's eyes brightened and she crossed her fingers. "Here's hoping!"

"And let's have a sleepover after," Cassandra said, reminding me of a fifth grader. "Just the four of us girls. We can have it at my house...if Bitchzilla agrees."

Spending the night at Cassandra's didn't sound very appealing. "Or we can have it here," I suggested.

Cassandra looked at Megan, and then shrugged. "You okay if Cait comes?"

"Of course." I was completely fine with Cait. After all, she hadn't done anything. "We just need to keep Kade off limits talk-wise."

"Agreed," Megan said, starting a clear coat. "My mum doesn't get off work until seven, so I'll be late to the game."

"We'll just meet you there," Cassandra said.

"Actually, I'll wait for you," I told Megan. In fact, showing up late and leaving early seemed like a good plan.

I opened the wrought iron gate to the cemetery and walked the long pathway to the mausoleum.

I needed to see Ian's grave. I'd wanted to visit for weeks, but today I had to. I felt drawn to it. A thousand different emotions washed through me as I scanned the area, and seeing the way clear, I removed the bolt cutters from where I'd hidden them inside my sweatshirt and cut the lock. I'd replace the lock tomorrow afternoon, after the slumber party.

I entered the mausoleum, shut the door behind me and went to Ian's grave.

"I miss you, Ian," I said under my breath, touching his gravestone, remembering the incredible time we'd had. God, how I wished for those summer days, for the easy friendship we had fallen into. For the intense conversations about life and death, and the spirit world. I had been one hundred percent myself and he hadn't judged me. Kind of like Kade. Which made sense since they were the same person.

I knew that with a certainty that surprised me. It was all beginning to come together. Laria's vendetta against me. It wasn't because I had crossed Ian over and broken the curse. Her fury was because Ian was back. He was Kade MacKinnon now, and just as Laria didn't want me with Ian then, she didn't want me with Kade now.

And she would do anything to keep us from being together.

Even if that meant killing me...or forcing us apart by other means.

Cruel, twisted bitch.

My cell rang, signaling I had a text.

Pick you up in five minutes.

I wasn't going to text Megan back and tell her to pick me up at the cemetery. I walked out of the mausoleum and looked toward the back stone wall of the cemetery. A blast of wind shot through me, and I lifted the hood over my hair and pulled the drawstrings tighter. I crossed my arms over my chest as I looked past the river.

I remembered reading the passage in the book Miss Akin had given me about Laria. That she'd been hanged from a tree at the castle and that her body was buried behind the cemetery on unhallowed ground. Across the river there was thick forestland. That forestland was close to the glen. I never got a warm and fuzzy feeling from the glen, that's for sure. In fact, I'd had a couple of Laria sightings there, and I'd also seen Randall, the creepy black magic guy.

My cell rang. I slid it out of my pocket. It was Megan. "Hey, where are you? I'm out front."

"You said you'd be five minutes."

"I figured we could stop at the store on the way to Reglin."

"Well, I'm at the cemetery."

She went silent for a few seconds and then said, "You must have hit your head really hard. That or you are completely mental."

"I'm mental," I said with a smile, and started walking back toward the front of the cemetery, ignoring the sensation of being flanked by ghosts on either side of me.

"I'll be right there...but I'm not coming in after you, so meet me at the front gate."

"I'm already headed in that direction." I clenched the bolt cutters tight in my fist, and picked up my pace. Within three more strides I felt the overwhelming sense to run come over me, but I kept my steps even.

"Riley."

I faltered when I heard my name called plain as day.

"Run Riley." My pulse leapt. It sounded like Anne Marie's voice.

From the corner of my eye I saw Laria...moving quickly from one tombstone to the next.

The wrought iron gate might as well have been a mile away. It seemed the faster I walked, the further away it got. I felt a piercing pain in the center of my back. Then another on my shin, and yet another on my shoulder. Laria was moving with me, her face inches from mine as her nails dug deeply into the back of my neck.

Megan pulled into the cemetery parking lot. I opened the gate and stepped out, wincing against the pain. I reached under my sweater and shirt and felt a welt against my fingers.

"Hey," I said, sliding into the passenger seat, trying to catch my breath. Laria had vanished. "Do you mind if we drop by the house? I forgot my purse."

"No problem," she said, looking past me toward the graveyard. "What were you doing in the cemetery?"

"I decided to take a walk. Too many days cooped up in the house, you know?"

She shook her head. "Actually, no, I don't know why you would want to take a walk in a graveyard of all places. That's just wrong."

We were at the inn in a minute, and I got out of the car and bolted up the steps. I lifted my shirt and looked in the mirror. Across my back there were three defined nail marks running down the entire length of my torso. The one on my leg wasn't as bad, but the one on my shoulder and neck had drawn blood. I put a bandage over it, and considered changing into something cuter than my Oregon Ducks hoodie, but decided against it since it hid the wounds really well.

The game had already started when we arrived. Cait, who had driven with Cassandra, motioned us over. I was happy to see Shane playing. My dad had told me earlier that he would try to make it, but I didn't see him in the stands, nor had I seen his car in the parking lot.

Shocker.

I tried to ignore the tall, handsome, dark-haired star player, but it was impossible. Gorgeous, ripped, and so athletic, he put every other player to shame. I kept thinking over what he'd said to me, the dream the night in Edinburgh, and Laria's vendetta. The pieces of the puzzle were fitting.

Kade kicked the ball straight to my brother, who in turn kicked it and scored the first goal. The crowd came to their feet and I was so happy for Shane.

Cassandra got on a roll with stories about her stepmother and the Italian gardener who was half her age. I didn't know if the stories were fact or fiction, but they were entertaining. So entertaining Megan snorted pop out her nose once, and she hit Cassandra like it was her fault.

We all laughed, and I even got the giggles. By the half, I was feeling more like my old self. When the teams headed off the field into the locker rooms Shane looked up at me and waved. I waved back... and so did all my friends.

I could feel Kade's gaze on me as he walked off the field.

"For what it's worth, he's happy you're here," Cait whispered under her breath, no doubt terrified to say the words too loud in case Cassandra heard. She'd been very careful not to say anything about Kade.

"We're headed to the bathroom. You want to come with?" Cassandra asked.

"No, go ahead," I said, having no desire to have another run-in with Laria in a bathroom. She'd proven she didn't care if she had an audience any longer.

The girls weren't gone two minutes when Madison slid onto the bench beside me. "Hey you."

Her hair was in a lopsided ponytail, and she wore two different colors of socks with pink sweats. "Hey. What have you been up to?"

"School and stuff." Fiddling with the charm bracelet at her wrist, she glanced up at me. "I heard you and Kade broke up."

The last thing I wanted or needed was to get into a conversation about Kade with his twelve-year-old cousin.

"I will never understand men. That's why I'll never have a boyfriend."

I had to laugh. I couldn't help it. She sounded wise beyond her years.

She actually scowled at me. "What are you laughing about?"

"No, nothing. You mean to tell me you're not crushing on any guy at school?"

Her brows furrowed. "No," she said a little too quickly. "Well, Andrew Donovan had a growth spurt over the summer, and he's so hot...but he doesn't know I exist."

"One day he will."

"How can you be so sure?" she asked.

"Because you're special."

She rolled her eyes.

"I'm not just saying that. You are special."

"We're special. Both of us, Ri...because we can both see spirits. Not everyone can, you know?"

How sweet. She was trying to make me feel better. "Yeah, I know." I wished I was one of those people who was in the majority and was oblivious that spirits walked the earth. My life would be a lot less complicated that way.

"Laria's dangerous, Riley. Much more dangerous than you know."

I knew exactly how dangerous she was, but I wasn't going to tell Madison about my experiences with Laria.

"Hanway says she's a master of deception. That she caused Kade to do some stuff he wouldn't normally do."

My heart pounded loud in my ears. "What stuff?"

"Like make Kade think he was with you when it was really Laria masquerading as you. She wanted everyone at the party to see Dana and Kade together, and for them to assume he was going out on you. So while everyone else was seeing Dana, Kade was seeing you."

She had just confirmed what I'd been wondering. "Hanway told you this?"

She nodded. "Yes, and he wants you to know the truth. He doesn't want Laria to win."

And that's exactly what she was doing...she was winning by keeping me and Kade apart.

"He says she can manipulate people," she said, and I could hear the fear in her voice. "Lots of people. She's strong and growing stronger by the day. She can take over a person...without that person realizing it. I mean, what will she do next?"

I'd been asking myself that same question for days. I thought of Shane telling me about his blackouts, and how his friends were telling him things he had done. Things he couldn't remember. Kind of like Kade...but Laria had gone a step further. She had made Kade believe he was with me that night of Tom's party. What else had she done to Kade, I wondered? Who else that I cared about had she messed with?

Madison glanced around and lowered her voice. "I'm scared for you, Riley."

I put an arm around her shoulder and gave her a hug, and she hugged me back.

My friends returned and Cait's brows furrowed as she looked at Madison. "What are you doing, squirt?"

Madison released me and stood. "Just sayin' hey. I'm gonna go now."

I grabbed her hand. "No, stay."

Madison glanced at Cait, who shrugged and gave Maddy's ponytail a playful tug. Megan sat down beside me, and Cait and Cassandra in front of us. The opposing team ran out on the field, and our players were right behind them.

My heart leapt at the sight of Kade. He had been played by Laria, just like I had been. We were both suffering because of her cruel acts, and Hanway was right...we couldn't let Laria win.

Once Kade got to the center of the field, he looked up at the stands, straight at me. This time I didn't look away. I smiled, and I saw the surprise on his face. His lips curved into a huge smile, and he didn't turn away until the referee blew the whistle signaling the game was starting.

Cait glanced back at me and grinned.

The second half flew by. Many of the students had left with fifteen minutes on the clock because our school was so far ahead. It was a blowout. Megan checked her watch. "We should head on out of here before the game ends. Maybe pick up a DVD for tonight."

"Sounds good," I said, ready to get home and hang out with my friends.

"We'll be there in about an hour, all right?" Cassandra said. "I have to stop by the house and pick up my jammies."

"You can always borrow some of mine," I said.

Cassandra's brows lifted. "Like I could fit into your skinny-ass pajamas. Thanks, but no thanks."

Cait laughed under her breath. "Maybe we'll snag a bottle of something from Bitchzilla while we're at it."

And after my conversation with Madison, I might just have a drink of whatever they brought back. "See you in a bit," I said, following behind Megan.

"He's looking for you," Megan said, eyes on the field. "Bloody hell, he's so obvious."

I could feel Kade's stare. I could feel him. Madison's words had given me a huge sense of relief, and now I knew for sure that Kade hadn't knowingly gone out on me with Dana. For the first time in days I felt like I could breathe.

Chapter Twenty-Six

We could hear the roar of the visitors' bleachers as we pulled onto the highway. "Kade MacKinnon does it again," Megan said with a laugh.

I smiled; I couldn't help it. Seeing him tonight had stirred up all the feelings I had for him. Now that I knew the truth about the night of Tom's party, I was ready to have a conversation with him. Maybe it was time for me to come clean about everything as well. To let him know about my abilities, about Laria, about Ian... even about cutting.

I glanced at Megan. "Thanks for taking me. I'm glad I came."

"I'm glad you did, too. You needed to get out of the house."

She wasn't kidding there. In the past few days the inn had become both a prison and a sanctuary. Dad had stayed close by, and Miss Akin even closer. I was relieved I had my friends staying with me tonight. I could use some comic relief.

My phone rang, signaling a text message. My heart leapt seeing Kade's number.

It was good to see you.

"Oh my God, is that Kade?" Megan asked in disbelief.

I nodded, pressing my lips together so I wouldn't smile.

She shook her head. "What do you want to bet that he's probably texting from the field."

I smiled at the image. I started to text back when she reached for my hand. "What are you doing? Give it a few minutes. Make him work for it, for God's sake."

The truth was…I didn't want to wait.

My phone rang again and Megan snorted.

"It's Shane."

Tell Miss A I'll be home late.

No mention of Dad. I couldn't blame him. Why hadn't he even attempted to make the game? It's not like it was that far from Braemar.

I typed back. *Will do! Congrats on the goal and the win!*

My phone rang.

Thanks! See you and the girls later.

I could see it already—my friends hanging out with Shane in his room, flirting like crazy with him. I shook my head and scrolled to Kade's text.

"You really like Kade, don't you?" Megan asked, her voice serious.

I glanced at her. "I love him."

Her eyes widened, but she didn't look all that surprised. "Wow, that's huge."

It was huge. Being with Kade felt right, and I wouldn't let Laria come between us again.

I chewed a fingernail as I stared at the cursor. I wanted to tell him that it was good to see him too…and so many other things, but I wasn't sure where to start.

I exhaled. My breath came out in a fog, and goosebumps rose on my flesh.

Megan's hand abruptly slapped over my wrist once again. Her hand was freezing cold.

My heart jumped in my chest. "Megan, what are you doing?"

Her hand squeezed tighter.

She turned to me and stared. There was nothing behind her eyes. Just a cold, dead expression on her face that terrified me.

"The road," I said, trying to jerk my hand away.

She held firm; a strong grip that shocked me.

"Watch the road, Megan!" I said, horrified and amazed when she took a corner without even looking at the road.

How the hell...

"Riley," she said, but it wasn't her voice, but rather a deep, creepy voice that shouldn't have come out of her.

Oh my God. I had nowhere to go, and Megan, or Laria, or whoever was in there, wasn't watching the road.

My hand was going numb. "Watch the road!"

A malevolent smile appeared on her lips as her head proceeded to turn toward the back of the car.

A horn blared as we came inches from the car that passed by us.

"Megan!!!!" I screamed.

She accelerated, and I gripped the dashboard with my free hand, listening with dread to the cracking and popping of her neck. The car veered off the road, into a fence and straight for a giant oak.

The wreck with my mom flashed before my eyes and I yelled, "Stop!"

Megan slammed on the brakes...but it was too late. We were going to collide with the tree.

I braced myself for the impact, but it never came. Instead the car abruptly screeched to a stop. Megan's head was resting against the steering wheel, her hair flung up and around it.

With shaky hands I unbuckled my seatbelt and reached for the door handle...just in case. "Megan?"

She moaned and lifted her head. I sighed in relief. She looked like Megan.

Blinking a few times, she glanced at the tree, then at me. "What happened?"

Was she serious?

"We ran off the road."

"Bloody hell." Unbuckling her seatbelt she scrambled out of the car and ran around to look at the damage. I was right behind her.

"Oh thank God," she said, putting a hand to her chest. The car was two inches from the tree. "I can't believe it. Look how close that is."

It was crazy close, and I knew someone was looking out for us. Someone had prevented us from hitting that tree. There was just no other explanation.

She stopped in her tracks. "Oh my God, you already have a concussion. Did you hit your head or anything?"

"No, I'm fine. I swear."

Sliding her hand down her face, she glanced at me, then at the car. "I don't remember anything before the wreck. I just remember leaving the game."

First it was Shane, then Kade, and now Megan.

I could feel cold all around us, and the breeze picked up. Being on an isolated stretch of road was nerve-wracking, especially with a maniacal ghost on the loose. "Let's get out of here. Do you want me to drive?"

She shook her head. "No, we'd both be in deep shit if you were caught driving without a license."

"Good point," I replied.

We got back in the car. She backed up but the car was stuck in the mud.

"Put it in gear. I'll get behind the car and push."

She rolled down her window. "Are you sure you don't want me to push and you drive?"

"Just drive," I said, the scratches on my body starting to burn again. Laria was relentless. I grit my teeth against the agonizing pain.

"Give it gas," I yelled.

Megan gunned it. I pushed with all my might, but the tires just spun in the mud. Seconds later I felt mud splatter against the entire right side of my body.

Great.

Megan looked in the side mirror. "Oh shit, I'm sorry, Ri!"

"Try it again."

This time she didn't hit the gas as hard, but it was clear we were making matters worse. The tires were sinking further into the mud.

I heard a car coming our way. Seeing a school bus, my heart missed a beat.

It passed by and every person on board was looking our way.

The football team.

The driver pulled over fifty yards up the road. The doors opened and the driver called out. "You need help?"

The words weren't out of his mouth before Shane wedged past him and ran toward us. "Are you guys okay?"

"Fine," we said at the same time.

Kade was on his heels. His gaze quickly assessed me from head to toe. "Are you all right?" I could see the concern in his eyes.

"We're fine."

"What happened?"

"We missed the turn."

"Apparently," Shane said, humor in his voice now that he could see we were okay. "You took out a good section of fence there, Meg."

"Just help push the car please," Megan said with a droll smile, getting back in the car.

Shane positioned himself behind the car. "Get inside with her," he said, sounding more like my dad than my brother. "MacKinnon and I will push."

"I can help push," I said, joining them.

"Riley, you have a concussion," Kade said. He reached up, brushed his fingers over my cheek. His lips curved softly. "You have mud all over you."

"Oh," I said, lifting my hand to feel for myself. Our fingers touched briefly. It might have been a small contact, but I felt it all the way to my toes.

"Riley, let's go," Megan said, her frustration obvious to everyone.

"I gotta go," I said, walking away. I slid into the passenger's seat.

Megan hit the gas, and the guys had us out in two seconds.

"Come on, lads!" the bus driver yelled. Curious onlookers had slowed, and traffic had backed up.

Kade stopped at my side of the window, his fingers gripping the door. "I need to talk to you, Ri. Please..."

I could see the desperation in his eyes and hear it in his voice.

"The girls are staying over tonight, so how about tomorrow?"

His shoulders sagged and he grinned, his relief obvious. "Name the time."

I bit my lower lip. "Um, how about I call you?"

By his expression, it wasn't the answer he wanted. "Promise you'll call, Riley?"

I slid my hand over his and squeezed it. "I promise. We have a lot to talk about."

Other books by J. A. Templeton

The Deepest Cut (a MacKinnon Curse novel, book one)

The Departed (a MacKinnon Curse novel, book three)

The MacKinnon Curse novella (The Beginning)

Acknowledgements

A HUGE thank you to my good friend and critique partner Patrice (P.T.) Michelle for your honest input on this story. You're a lifesaver.

Thanks to Pam Berehulke for your wonderful edit. You pointed out so many helpful things.

Thank you to the reviewers and readers who enjoyed The Deepest Cut. I appreciate your support more than you'll ever know.

Last, but certainly not least, thanks to my wonderful husband, who puts up with late dinners and quiet nights when I'm on deadline...or when I just can't seem to pull myself away from my imaginary world & characters.

About the Author

J.A. Templeton writes young adult novels featuring characters that don't necessarily fit into any box. Aside from writing and reading, she enjoys research, traveling, riding motorcycles, and spending time with family and friends. Married to her high school sweetheart, she has two grown children and lives in Washington. Visit her website www.jatempleton.com for the most updated information on new releases. She loves hearing from readers!